'My name is C

DeSanquez, DeSanquez... Annie was thinking frowningly. And then it hit—with a sickening sense of understanding that made her sway where she stood.

'Ah,' he murmured. 'I see you are beginning to catch on. You made the quick connection, I must assume, because your...affair with my brother-in-law took place in the DeSanquez apartment. The media made quite a meal out of these juicy facts, did they not? They told of Annie Lacey lying with her lover in one bed, while her lover's wife lay asleep in another bedroom in the same apartment. My apartment, Miss Lacey,' he enunciated thinly. 'My bed!'

Michelle Reid grew up on the southern edges of Manchester, the youngest in a family of five lively children. But now she lives in the beautiful county of Cheshire with her busy executive husband and two grown-up daughters. She loves reading, the ballet, and playing tennis when she gets the chance. She hates cooking, cleaning, and despises ironing! Sleep she can do without, and produces some of her best written work during the early hours of the morning.

Recent titles by the same author:

THE ULTIMATE BETRAYAL

THE MORNING AFTER

BY
MICHELLE REID

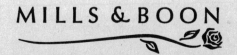

All the characters in this book have no existence outside the imagination of the author, and have no relation whatsoever to anyone bearing the same name or names. They are not even distantly inspired by any individual known or unknown to the author, and all the incidents are pure invention.

© Michelle Reid 1996

ISBN 0 263 79510 1

*Set in Times Roman 10 on 11¼ pt.
01-9606-51490 C1*

Made and printed in Great Britain

CHAPTER ONE

ANNIE wanted to scream. She *tried* to scream! But every time she opened her mouth he covered it with his own.

It was horrible. A violation. She felt sick.

And it was dark in the room—very dark. The air hot and stifling, filled with the laboured breathing of their uneven struggle. Hands grappling against intrusive hands—her strangled sobs mingling with his thick, excited groans. Alien sounds, smells and textures swamping her senses to hold her trapped in a terrifyingly black void of wretched helplessness.

Suffocating—she felt as if she was suffocating. She couldn't breathe. She couldn't think beyond that vile, thrusting tongue. She could feel her heart pounding in wild fear. It throbbed in her chest, her head—thundered in her ears.

Her clothes had gone. She didn't know where or even how they had gone—but they were no longer covering her body.

Louis Alvarez was. Big, strong and repulsively naked. His greedy hands touching everywhere—*everywhere*.

It didn't help that she was slightly drunk from the amount of champagne that she had swallowed. She felt weak and dizzy, her head swimming as she tossed it from side to side in an effort to evade his awful mouth.

He dealt with this by reaching out to grasp a fistful of her silken gold hair, using it to clamp her twisting head to the bed. Her whimper of pain brought his smothering mouth back onto hers.

And then the real nightmare began.

5

His free hand, shifting to cover one madly palpitating breast, moulding, squeezing before moving on, palm sliding over quivering flesh, eager, hungry. Fingers searching, probing, hurting until, on a sudden surge of sexual urgency, he thrust a knee between her thighs and wedged them wide apart.

Then he was there, heavy on her, his mouth dragging sideways away from hers on a rasping sigh of pleasure as his swollen manhood made contact with her warm flesh.

And at last from somewhere—from nowhere—she didn't know where—she found the ability to scream. Her body arching away from the invading thrust of his body, her slender neck arching away from the sickening threat of his thrusting tongue—

Then a door was opening, a burst of light flooding like acid through her tortured mind. And the scream came, thick and wretched—a cry from hell, filling the air around her...

The flash bulbs began popping even before the limousine drew to a halt outside the hotel. Annie Lacey and Todd Hanson were big news at the moment. And the paparazzi were out in force.

The car stopped, a uniformed attendant stepped forward to open a door and the flash bulbs went wild, catching frame by frame the appearance of a strappy gold shoe and one long, long silk-clad female leg. Then a head appeared, breast-length, die-straight wheat-blonde hair floating around a physically perfect female face, followed by the rest of the exquisite creature, wearing nothing more than a shimmering short scrap of pure white silk that seemed held to her body only by the thin gold belt she had cinched into her narrow waist.

Annie Lacey. Tall, blonde and leggy. A lethal combination. Beautiful, with a pair of cool, cool pure blue eyes which were so disconcertingly at odds with her shockingly sensual siren's mouth. She was the present-day super-sought-after supermodel. And super-tramp to those who believed slavishly every word printed by the tabloid Press.

They envied her, though. Love or despise her for her morals, they envied her how she looked and what those looks had brought her.

Fame. Fortune.

Gods, to a lot of people. Unreachable dreams to most. To Annie herself?

Well, she used that gorgeous mouth to smile for the cameras while those blue eyes gave nothing away of what was going on behind them. What Annie thought or felt about most things was kept a close secret—which was why the Press had such a field-day where she was concerned. They could say and print what they liked about her, safe in the knowledge that she wouldn't retaliate.

Smile and say nothing, was her motto. Because whatever you did say would be taken down and twisted into something completely different—mainly something more likely to sell papers. And that meant lies, sex and the inevitable scandal—a lesson she had once learned the hard way.

A man—a big, blond-haired, blue-eyed man who was as handsome as she was beautiful—rounded the car to arrive at her side, and instantly the media interest intensified.

'Mr Hanson—Mr Hanson! It is true that Annie got the *Cliché* contract as a direct result of her relationship with you?'

Todd's hand settled about Annie's waist, drawing her close as the next question hit.

'Are you lovers, Mr Hanson?'

'Will Susie Frazer return to the States now she's lost both you and the *Cliché* contract, Mr Hanson?'

'Is there any truth in the rumour that Miss Frazer dumped you because you refused to dump Miss Lacey?'

'I hate you for setting us both up for this,' Annie threw at Todd through gritted teeth.

'Just keep smiling and ignore them,' was all he replied, pressing her into motion towards the hotel. 'They're just fishing. They don't really know anything.'

'What, with Susie feeding them their lines?' she drawled.

'She's a bitch,' he allowed, 'but not that big a bitch.'

'Was that a joke?' Annie mocked him. 'She's out for blood. My blood preferably.'

'I wish you two could have become friends,' he sighed as they stepped through the hotel doors.

'And pigs might fly,' was her only reply to that.

There never had been any love-loss in evidence between the two top models from the moment they'd first met. That had been just over six months ago, when Susie Frazer had come to London from her native Los Angeles to attend the British Advertising Awards.

Annie had been there with Todd that time too, he in his role as head of Hanson Publications and more specifically as representative of *Cliché* magazine—one of the top British monthly glossies on the present-day market—and Annie because she was featured in that month's issue of *Cliché* wearing that season's latest from the Paris shows.

Susie had taken one look at the dynamically handsome Todd Hanson and fallen like a ton of bricks—had seen that he had none other than the notorious Annie Lacey hanging on his arm and declared outright war on the spot.

'Who does she think she is, looking at you as if you're dirt?' Todd had demanded furiously.

'My reputation goes before me, darling,' she'd drawled mockingly in reply. 'But, you have to admit, she does look rather spectacular glaring at me like that.'

Tall and reed-thin, the brilliant flame of her gorgeous red hair forming the most wonderful halo of fire around her exquisite face, spectacular Susie certainly had looked. And despite his anger Annie had been able to tell by the sudden gleam in his eye that Todd had thought so too. So she hadn't been that surprised to discover a few weeks later that Susie had moved into Todd's apartment with him.

LUCKY DEVIL HANSON HAS THE PICK OF THE CROP! the tabloids had read that week, featuring accompanying photos of Todd with Annie and Todd with Susie, both women gazing adoringly into his handsome face. Annie had thought it rather amusing, but Susie hadn't. She was spoiled, vain, jealous and possessive. And she wanted Annie cut right out of Todd's life. The fact that she had never managed to achieve this aim made her animosity towards Annie almost palpable. So when Annie had been chosen over Susie to promote *Cliché's* launch into Europe earlier this week Susie had retaliated by walking out on Todd.

Which was why Annie was here tonight with Todd, instead of Susie. He was still stinging from the way that Susie had walked out on him, and his self-esteem had hit rock-bottom. He needed a beautiful woman hanging on his arm to bolster his ego and—no vanity intended— Annie was undoubtedly it!

'Susie will be there,' he'd said, explaining his reason for wanting her here with him tonight. 'She's accused me often enough of having something going with you. So let her think she was right! It will certainly hit her where it will hurt her the most—in her over-suspicious little mind!'

It hadn't been the best incentive that Annie had ever been offered to attend something she did not want to go to. But what the heck? she'd decided ruefully; her own reputation had been shot to death years ago when she'd been named as the other woman in the much publicised Alvarez divorce. And Annie owed Todd—owed him a lot for bringing her through that wretched ordeal a reasonably sane woman.

Like the rock she had always likened him to. Todd had stood by her right through it all, not caring if some of her dirt rubbed off on him. But, most precious of all, he'd believed her—believed her in the sight of so much damning evidence against her, and for that she would always be grateful. Grateful enough to do anything for him—even play the outright vamp if he asked it of her.

Which was exactly what she was here to do. But...

'Just remember I'm here only as a big favour to you,' she reminded him as they paused in the open doorway to the huge reception room to take in the glittering array of those already gathered there, who were considered best and most powerful in the advertising fraternity. 'Once I'm sure Susie has taken note that we are a pair I'm off home. I hate these kinds of do's.'

But, champagne glass in hand, she moved with Todd from group to group, smiling, chatting, smoothly fielding the light and sometimes not so light banter came their way, and generally giving the impression that she was thoroughly enjoying herself, while her eyes kept a sharp look-out for Susie.

It was then that she felt it—a sharp, tingling sensation in her spine that caught at her breath and made her spin quickly to search out the originator of the red-hot needles at present impaling themselves in her back.

She expected to see Susie. In fact, she had been so sure it would be Susie that it rather disconcerted her to find herself staring across the crowded room at not a

red-haired witch with murderous green eyes but a man.
A strange man. The most darkly attractive man she had
ever encountered in her life before.

Dressed in a conventional black bow-tie and dinner
suit, he stood a good head and shoulders taller than
anyone else. His hair was black—an uncompromising
raven-black, dead straight and shiny, scraped severely
back from a lean, darkly tanned face. A riveting face.
A face with eyes that seemed to be piercing right into
her from beneath the smooth black brows he had lowered
over them. Thin nose, straight, chiseled mouth and
chin—he had the haughty look of a Spanish conquistador about him. And he possessed the neat, tight body
of a dancer, slim but muscled, lithe like a dancer—a
Spanish dancer, she found herself extending hectically.

Something like a small explosion of feeling took place
deep inside her stomach, and hurriedly she looked away,
going to wind herself closer to Todd, as though his re-
assuring bulk could soothe the disturbing sensation away.

'What's the matter with you?' Todd murmured,
turning from the conversation he was having with a
couple of business cronies to frown at the way she was
suddenly clinging to his arm.

'Nothing,' she denied, feeling decidedly agitated.
'Where's Susie?' she snapped with a sudden impatience.
'I would have thought she'd have shown her face by now.'

Todd smiled—a thin, hard parody of a smile. 'She's
over there,' he said, nodding his head in the direction
in which Annie had just seen the stranger. 'Playing vamp
to that guy from the Rouez Sands Group.'

'Who—Josh Tulley?'

'Mmm,' he confirmed, hiding his jealousy behind that
casual reply.

But Annie wasn't fooled. She knew how crazy Todd
was about Susie. She knew how much this was hurting
him, and her eyes clouded in gentle sympathy. 'You have

been living like man and wife for the last six months, darling,' she reminded softly. 'Maybe she has a right to feel rejected by you over this *Cliché* thing.'

If Annie had been hoping that her defence of Susie would help soften his heart towards the woman he loved, it didn't. If anything it only helped to annoy him. 'I'm a businessman, not a pimp,' he clipped. 'My boardroom is not in my bedroom. She knew that before she decided to try her luck in either.'

But that is not what the papers are saying, is it? Annie contemplated heavily. And once again it would be Annie Lacey who was going to carry the mucky can. Then she was instantly disgusted with herself for worrying about her own bad press when Todd had not worried about the mud thrown at him during her fall from grace four years ago!

'Love you,' she murmured softly, and reached up to press a tender kiss to his cheek.

Then she almost fell over when those red-hot needles returned with a vengeance. They prickled her spine, raising the fine, silken hairs on the back of her neck, drying her mouth, tightening tiny muscles around her lungs so that she found breathing at all an effort.

She must have actually stumbled because suddenly Todd exclaimed, 'What the hell—?' He made a grab to steady her, his blue eyes narrowing into a puzzled frown as he peered down into her unusually flushed face. 'Are you tipsy?' he demanded, sounding almost shocked.

It was a shock she well understood. Todd knew as well as Annie did that she had not consumed more than half a glass of anything alcoholic in any one evening in over four years.

Not since the Alvarez affair, in fact.

She shuddered on the name. 'No. I just feel a bit flushed, that's all.' Hamming it up, she began fanning herself with a hand. 'It's so damned hot in here. Oh, look! There's Lissa!' she cried, wanting to divert him. Why, she wasn't sure. 'I'll leave you to your boring businessmen and go and have a chat. Is Susie still in evidence?'

Todd glanced over Annie's shoulder then away again swiftly. 'Yes,' he said, and she could tell by the sudden tensing of his jaw that he hadn't liked what he'd seen.

'Then I want a kiss,' Annie commanded, reaching up to wind her arms around his neck.

He grinned, relaxing again, and gave it.

'Take that, you bitch,' she murmured to the unseen Susie as they drew apart.

Todd shook his head with a wry smile of appreciation for the act that she was putting on for him. 'You,' he murmured, 'are a dangerous little witch, Annie Lacey.'

'Because I love you and don't mind showing it?' she questioned innocently.

'No,' he chuckled. 'Because you love me one way but enjoy presenting it in another. Now, stop laying it on with a trowel and go and talk to Lissa.'

He gave her a light tap on her rear to send her on her way and she fluttered her lashes at him as she went, his laughter following behind her.

The sound was like manna from heaven to Annie, who hadn't heard him laugh like that in days. And she decided it was worth all the speculative looks that she was now receiving from those around them who had witnessed their little staged scene just to know that he had got his sense of humour back.

And that included the dark, brooding look that she was receiving from one man in particular, she noted on a sudden return of that hot breathlessness.

He was now standing on the other side of the room— though how he'd got there that quickly through this crush Annie didn't know.

Her heart skipped a beat.

That look was very proprietorial.

Who did he think he was, looking at her like that?

Her chin came up, her famous, cool blue eyes challenging him outright.

He smiled, his chiselled mouth twisting wryly, and he gave a small shrug of one broad shoulder as if to say, I have no right but—what the hell?

Arrogant devil! With a toss of her beautiful hair she spun away and went to join her agent. But right through the next half-hour she was acutely aware of him, what he was doing and who he was talking to.

And even more acutely aware of every time his glance came her way.

It was weird, oddly threatening yet disturbingly intimate.

Todd joined her, and after a short while they moved off through the crush, eyes with varying expressions following their slow progress as they paused several times to speak to people they knew. Some envied Todd Hanson the delicious woman curved to his side, and some envied her the attractive man she was with. But few could deny that they complemented each other perfectly—she with her long, softly rounded, very feminine body, he with his tightly packed, muscled frame, both with their fair-skinned, blond-haired, aggravatingly spectacular looks.

They ended up in another room where a buffet had been laid out. It was the usual kind of spread expected at these functions—finger food, high on calories and low on appetite satisfaction. Todd loaded up a plate with Annie's help, then they found a spot against a wall to share their spread, the plate full of food balanced between them on the flat of Todd's palm.

It all looked very cosy, very intimate, with Todd feeding Annie her favourite devilled prawns while she held a chicken drumstick up for him to bite into. But the conversation between them was far from cosy.

'Well, did you get to speak to her?' Annie asked him bluntly.

'She collared me.' Todd shrugged offhandedly. 'It wasn't the other way around.'

'After waiting until I was safely out of the way, of course. Bite—you've missed a tasty bit there...' He bit, sharp white teeth slicing easily into succulent chicken. 'So, what did she have to say?'

Another shrug. 'Nothing worth repeating,' he dismissed.

Which meant, Annie surmised, that Susie had spent the time she'd had alone with him slaying Annie's character. He fed her a mushroom-filled canapé and she chewed on it thoughtfully for a while, then said firmly, 'All right, tell me what you said to her, then.'

For a moment his eyes twinkled, wry amusement putting life into the pure blue irises. 'Just like that,' he murmured ruefully. 'She could just have been enquiring about your health, you know.'

'And we both know she was not,' Annie drawled.

He huffed out a short laugh. 'Do you have any false illusions about yourself at all, Annie?' he asked curiously.

'None that I know of.' She pouted, then, like him, shrugged a slender shoulder. 'They wouldn't be much use to me if I did have them, would they?' She was referring to the fact that people believed what they were conditioned to believe, and the Alvarez affair had done the conditioning on her character four years ago.

His blue eyes clouded at her candid honesty about herself, a grim kind of sympathy replacing the moment's amusement. 'I wish...' he began, but she stopped him by placing sticky fingers over his lips.

'No,' she said, her eyes suddenly dark and sombre. 'No wishes. No heart-searching or self-recriminations. They serve no useful purpose. And we know what we are to each other, no matter what everyone else wants to believe.'

'I love you,' he murmured, and kissed the tips of her fingers where they lay lightly against his mouth.

'Now that,' she decided, 'has just earned you the right to use me whenever you want to. Business or pleasure, my love. I am at your service!'

A sudden movement on the very periphery of her vision had her head twisting in that direction just in time to catch sight of her stranger turning away from them, and that odd feeling went chasing down her spine again.

'Have you any idea who that man is?' she asked Todd.

'Which one?' he prompted, glancing in the direction that she was looking, but already the stranger had disappeared through the door which led into the main function room.

'It doesn't matter.' She turned back to face Todd. 'He's gone.' And she made a play of cleaning her sticky fingers on the damp towels provided, aware that Todd was frowning at her, wondering why she'd felt driven to remark on the person at all. He knew that it wasn't like her; she usually showed a distinct lack of interest in the male sex in general. So her sudden interest in one man in particular intrigued him. But just when he was going to quiz her further a colleague of his joined them, and the moment was lost.

A fact for which Annie was thankful, because she didn't think that she could give Todd a reason why the stranger was bothering her as much as he was. He was impertinent, certainly. The way he had been watching her all evening made him that. And arrogant too, because he didn't even bother to look away when she caught him doing it!

But...

She had no answer to her 'but'. And on a sudden burst of restlessness she excused herself from Todd and his companion with the excuse that she was going to the bathroom.

She began threading her way through the crowd towards the main foyer, a tall, graceful mover with the kind of figure that was now back in fashion—slender but curvy, with high, firm breasts, a narrow waist and sensually rounded hips.

Being so blonde meant that the white and gold combination of her outfit suited her, the silk clinging sensually as she walked, advertising the distinct lack of underwear beneath it. But although she was well aware of the admiring glances that she was receiving she acknowledged few of them, smiling only at people she knew but giving them no chance to waylay her.

The foyer was almost as busy as the function rooms, with people milling about or just standing in small groups chatting, and Annie paused by the doorway, her blue gaze searching for the direction of the ladies' room. She spied it way across on the other side of the thickly carpeted foyer, but had barely taken a small step in that direction when she caught a flashing glimpse of flamered hair and sighed when she realised that Susie was going in the same direction.

In no mood for a cat-fight in the Ladies, she watched Susie disappear from view, then turned, feeling a bit at a loss as to what to do next and wondering if she dared just walk out of here without telling Todd.

She'd had enough now and wanted to go home. The tall dark stranger had unsettled her. And the fact that Todd had already had his confrontation with Susie, and that Susie was completely aware of whom Todd was here with, made her reasons for being here at all redundant.

And, to be honest, her bed beckoned. In her line of business early nights were a fact of life, and her body clock was telling her that she was usually tucked up and fast asleep by now.

Quite how it happened she didn't know, but all of a sudden a noisy group came bursting out of the room she'd just left, forcing her to take a quick step back out of their way—which brought her hard up against the person standing behind her.

She turned quickly to apologise—only to stiffen on a fiercely indrawn breath as something icy cold and very wet landed against her chest . . . !

CHAPTER TWO

'*Oh*...!' she gasped out shrilly.

'Damn,' a deep voice muttered. 'My apologies.'

But Annie was too busy trying to catch her breath to listen to any apology as she watched what looked like the full contents of a tall, fluted glass of champagne drip down the honeyed slopes of her breasts. Ice-cold bubbles were fizzing against her heated skin, the chilled liquid soaking into the thin white silk of her bodice.

The fabric darkened, then turned transparent before her very eyes, plastering itself so tightly to her breasts that anyone within a vicinity of ten feet would now know that she was definitely not wearing a bra! And to top that humiliating exposure her nipples, always so annoyingly sensitive to quick changes in temperature, burst into tight, prominent buds, pushing against the wet fabric in sheer, affronted surprise!

'Hell,' the culprit muttered, making her wretchedly aware that he was seeing exactly what she was seeing—and from a better vantage point than anyone else, including herself. In a delayed act of modesty she snapped her arms across her breasts at the same time as her head came up to receive the second stunning shock in as many seconds.

It was the man who had been watching her all evening—the same man who had filled her with such strange, unsettling feelings—and she just stared at him blankly, her lovely mouth parted while her body quivered badly enough for anyone to see that she was suffering from a severe state of shock.

Then flash bulbs began to pop, and the next thing she knew a male chest of a rock-like substance was blocking her off from view as a strong arm whipped around her waist to pull her hard up against his muscle-packed frame.

'Pretend you know me!' he muttered urgently. And before she could begin to think what he meant his mouth took fierce possession of her own.

Annie froze, this shock invasion, coming on top of all the other shocks she had just received, holding her so stiff and still that she simply let him get away with it!

But the shock did not stop her from being intensely aware of the way his mouth seemed to burn against her own, or the way he was holding her so tightly that her wet breasts were being crushed against the silky fabric of his dinner jacket. And she could feel his breath warm against her cheek, smell the slightly spicy scent of him that teased her stammering senses.

She was panting for breath by the time he drew away, giving only enough space between their lips so he could speak to her softly and swiftly. 'At the moment only you and I know about the champagne.' His voice held the finest hint of an accent—American tinged with something else... 'Keep up the pretence of knowing me and those greedy cameras will merely believe that Annie Lacey has just been greeted by one of her many lovers. You understand?'

Many lovers? She blinked, still too shocked, too bewildered by a mad set of events to begin to think clearly.

Then more flash bulbs popped, and she closed her eyes as tomorrow's headlines played their acid taunt across the inside of her lids: Annie Lacey Bares All in Champagne Clash!

'Oh, God,' she whispered shakily.

He shifted slightly, accepting her response as acknowledgement of his advice, a large hand splaying across the base of her spine to ease her more closely to him. 'Smile,' he instructed brusquely.

Obediently she fixed a tight, bright smile to her throbbing lips.

'Now reach up and kiss me in return.'

Her eyes widened, then darkened in dumb refusal. He read it, and his own eyes flashed a warning. Green, she realised quite out of context. His eyes were green.

'Do it!' he commanded harshly. 'Do it, you fool, if you want this to look natural!'

More flash bulbs popped, congealing the horror in her shock-paralysed throat when she realised that her choices were few. She either complied with this frightening man's instructions or she faced the humiliation that she would receive at the hands of the gutter Press.

It was no contest really, she decided bleakly. The Press would be cruel—too cruel. This man—this frightening stranger—could never hurt her as deeply as a ruthless Press could do.

So with a dizzy sense of unreality washing numbly through her, her eyes clinging like confused prisoners to the glinting urgency in his, her tense fingers began sliding up his chest and over his broad shoulders, and her slender body stretched up along the ungiving length of his as she went slowly up on tiptoe to bring her reluctant mouth into contact with his.

Only, her mouth never made it as she received yet another shock—a shock which made her wet breasts heave against his hard chest in surprise, and sent her blue eyes wider, her quivering mouth too—when her fingers made accidental contact with something at his nape.

His hair was so long that he had it tied back with a thin velvet ribbon!

He gave a soft laugh deep in his throat, white teeth flashing between beautifully moulded lips, sardonically smiling in amusement at her shock.

Then he wasn't smiling, his green eyes darkening into something that stung her with a hot, dark sense of her own femininity and had her body stiffening in rejection even as he arched her up against him and closed the gap between their mouths.

She stopped breathing. Her fingers coiled tensely around that long, sleek tail of dark, silken hair as fine, pulsing jets of stinging, hot awareness sprayed heat across her trembling flesh.

For all her carefully nurtured reputation, for all the juicy rumours about her personal life, Annie rarely allowed herself to be properly kissed, rarely let any man close enough to try—though those who wished to would rather have died than admit such a thing to anyone, which was why her image as a man-killer stayed so perfectly intact.

So to have this man kiss her—not superficially but with enough sensual drive to have her own lips part to welcome him—seemed to throw her into a deeper state of shock, holding her completely still in his arms as she felt her response like a lick of fire burning from mouth to breasts then, worse, to the very core of her sex. Her muscles contracted fiercely in reaction, her lips quivering on yet another helpless gasp.

Then, thankfully, she was free—thankfully because in all her life she had never experienced a response like that! And the fact that she had done so with this perfect stranger both frightened and bewildered her.

'Right,' he muttered. 'Let's get the hell out of here.'

Crazily she found herself leaning weakly against him, sponge-kneed and dizzy with the strange cacophony of reactions taking place inside her. Her mouth was throbbing, her heart trembling and her damp breasts quivering where they were being pressed tightly against his chest.

Inside she was fainting—it was the only way her muzzy head could think of describing that odd, dragging feeling that seemed to be trying to sink her like liquid to the ground. Even the roots of her hair reacted stingingly as his chin brushed across the top of her head when he moved to glance around them.

He shifted her beneath the crook of his powerful arm, and he was big—big enough to fit her easily beneath his shoulder, even though she was no small thing herself. Her hand slid from the long lock of his hair to flutter delicately down his back to his lean, tight waist, her other pressing against the front of his white dress shirt where she was made forcefully aware of the accelerated pounding of his heart beneath the sticky dampness where her wetness had transferred itself to him.

The whole scene must have looked powerfully emotional to anyone watching all of this take place— the notorious Annie Lacey meeting, throwing herself upon and leaving hurriedly with a man who could only be an old and very intimate friend by the way he held her clasped so possessively to him. But, huddled against him as she was, at that moment she could only be glad of his powerful bulk because it helped to hide what had happened to her from all those curious eyes.

But when she felt the cooling freshness of the summer night air hit her body she at last made an effort to pull her befuddled brain together.

'Wait a minute!' she gasped, pulling to a dead stop in front of the row of waiting black cabs. 'I—'

'Just get in,' he instructed, transferring his grip to her elbow and quite forcefully propelling her inside the nearest cab.

Annie landed with less than her usual grace on the cheap, cracked leather seat.

'What the hell do you think you're doing?' she exclaimed with shrill indignity as he climbed right in behind her.

He didn't bother to answer, but instead, and to her horror, began stripping off his black silk evening jacket!

Annie made an ungainly scramble into the furthest corner of the seat, blue eyes revealing the real alarm she was now beginning to feel.

'Where to, mate?'

'Tell the guy,' the man beside her commanded. 'Then put that on—' the jacket landed on her trembling lap '—before his eyes pop out of his head.'

Annie glanced sharply at the cabby to find his eyes fixed on her breasts so shockingly outlined against the sodden fabric of her dress. Dark heat stung along her cheeks as hurriedly she dragged the jacket around her slender shoulders and clutched possessively at its black satin lapels.

'Your address,' her accoster prompted, after having watched sardonically her rush to cover herself up.

Annie flashed him a fulminating look, frustratedly aware that she had no choice but to comply. Well, she did have a choice, she acknowledged bitterly. She could toss this alarming man back his jacket, climb out of the cab and walk back into the hotel to face all those eagerly speculative eyes while she went in search of Todd.

But the very idea of doing that made her feel slightly sick. All those eyes with their amused, knowing looks, and sly sniggers from people who would see the whole thing as yet another Annie Lacey sensation.

Reluctantly she muttered her address, then subsided stiffly into her corner of the cab while he leaned forward to repeat it to the cabby.

Annie followed the lithe movement of his long body with her eyes.

Who is he? she wondered tensely. Though he sounded American there was an added hint of a foreign accent in his deep, gravelly voice that she couldn't quite place. And his skin wore a rich, smooth olive tint that suggested foreign climes—like the colour of his raven-black hair with its outrageous pony-tail lying smoothly along the pure silk of his bright white dress shirt between well-muscled shoulderblades.

What is he? Even in profile his face showed a hard-boned toughness of character that somehow did not go with the flamboyant style of his hair.

He gave a conflict of impressions, she realised, and wondered if it was a deliberately erected façade aimed to put people off the track where his true personality was concerned.

And why did she think that? Because she did it herself and therefore could recognise the same trait in others.

Instruction to the cabby completed, he slid the partitioning window shut then sat back to look at her.

Instantly those strange sparks of awareness prickled along the surface of her skin—an awareness of his firm, sculptured mouth that had so shockingly claimed her own, of lips that made hers tingle in memory, made her throat go dry as they stretched into a smooth, mocking smile.

'A novel way of meeting, don't you think?' he drawled.

Not gravel but velvet. She found herself correcting her description of the liquid tones of his voice. And laced with a hint of—what? Contempt? Sarcasm? Or just simple, wry amusement at the whole situation? Annie flicked her wary glance up to his eyes. Strange eyes. Green. Green eyes that again did not go with the dark Latin rest of him, and were certainly alight with something that kept her senses alert to the threat of danger.

Danger?

'You were watching me earlier,' she said half-accusingly. 'And you know my name.'

He smiled at that, the wry—yes, it was wry—amusement deepening in his eyes. 'But you are a very beautiful woman, Miss Lacey,' he pointed out. 'Your face and your body can be seen plastered on billboards all over the world. Of course I know your name.' He gave a small shrug of those wide, white-clad shoulders. 'I would expect every red-blooded man alive to recognise you on sight.'

'Except that all those other men do not make a point of stalking me all evening,' she pointed out.

His attention sharpened. 'Are you by any chance trying to imply something specific?' he enquired carefully.

Was she? She was by nature very suspicious of men in general. This one seemed to have gone out of his way to be where he was right now.

'Perhaps you suspect me of spilling the champagne deliberately?' he suggested, when Annie did not say anything.

'Did you?' Cool blue eyes threw back a challenge.

He smiled—the kind of noncommittal smile that tried to mock her for even thinking such a thing about him. But she was not convinced by it, or put off.

'Things like it have happened before,' she told him. 'In my business you collect nut cases like other people collect postage stamps.'

'And you see me as the ideal candidate for that kind of weird behaviour?' He looked so amused by the idea that it made her angry.

'You can't tell by just looking at them, you know,' she snapped. 'They don't have ''crazy man'' stamped on their foreheads to give me a clue.'

'But in your business, Miss Lacey, you must surely accept that kind of thing as merely par for the course.'

'And therefore relinquish the right to care?'

He offered no answer to that, but his eyes narrowed thoughtfully on her as though he was making a quick reassessment of something he had already set in his mind about her, and a small silence fell.

Annie turned her head away to stare out the cab window so that she did not have to try and read what that reassessment was about. Why, she wasn't sure, except...

She sighed inwardly. She knew why. She'd looked away because he disturbed her oddly. His dark good looks disturbed her. The way he had been staring at her earlier disturbed her. His shocking kisses had disturbed her, awakening feelings inside her that she had honestly believed she did not possess.

The black cab rumbled on, stopping and starting in London's busy night traffic. People were out in force, the warm summer night and the fact that it was tourist season in the city filling the streets with life. Pub doors stood wedged open to help ease the heated air inside rooms packed with casually dressed, enviably relaxed people. Cafés with their pavements blocked continental-style by white plastic tables had busy waiters running to and fro, and the sights and smells and sounds were those of a busy international metropolis, all shapes, sizes, colours and creeds mingling in a mad, warm bustle of easy harmony.

She sighed softly to herself, wishing that she could be like them, wishing that she could walk out and mingle inconspicuously with the crowd and just soak up some of that carefree atmosphere. But she couldn't. Her looks were her fortune, and therefore were too well-known— as the man sitting beside her had just pointed out. Dressed in jeans and a T-shirt with a scarf covering her head, she would still be recognised. She knew because she'd tried it.

The trouble was, she decided heavily, she was becoming weary of the life she led, the restrictions that life placed on her. Tired of an image that she had created for herself which meant her always having to be on her guard with people—people like the man sitting beside her.

'The champagne caught your hair.' The sudden touch of light fingers on a sticky tendril of hair just by her left ear had Annie reacting instinctively.

She jerked violently away from his touch. He went very still, his strange eyes narrowing on her face with an expression that she found difficult to define as he slowly lowered his hand again, long, blunt-ended fingers settling lightly on his own lap.

A new silence began to fizz between them, and Annie did not know what to say to break it. There was something about this man that frightened her—no matter how much she tried to tell herself that she was being paranoid about him. Even that touch—that light, innocent brush of his fingers against her hair—had filled her with the most incredible alarm. Her heart was hammering too, rattling against her ribs with enough force to restrict her breathing.

She bit down on her lower lip, even white teeth pressing into lush, ruby-coloured flesh, and her dusky lashes lowered to hide her discomfort as warm colour began to seep into her cheeks.

Then the cab made a sharp turn, and she saw with relief that they were turning into a narrow cobbled street of pretty, whitewashed cottages, one of which was her own.

Almost eagerly she shifted towards the edge of the seat so that she could jump out just as soon as they stopped. The sound of soft laughter beside her made her throw a wary glance at her companion.

He was smiling, ruefully shaking his sleek dark head. 'I am not intending to jump on you, you know,' he drawled. 'I assure you I do possess a little more finesse than to seduce my women in the back seats of black cabs. And,' he went on, before Annie could think of a thing to say in reply, 'I did think my behaviour exemplary enough to give me gallant-knight status if nothing else.'

He thought those kisses in the hotel foyer exemplary behaviour? She didn't. And he could sit there smiling that innocently mocking smile as long as he wanted to, but she would not lower her guard to him. Her senses were just too alert to the hidden danger in him to do that.

'I'm sorry,' she said coolly. 'But gallant knights are so few and far between that a girl does not expect to meet one these days.'

The taxi came to a stop outside her tiny mews cottage then—thankfully. Because she was suddenly very desperate to get away from this strange, disturbing man.

But as she went to slip off his jacket and opened her mouth to utter some polite little word of thanks for his trouble he stopped her.

'No.' His hand descended onto her shoulder to hold his jacket in place. 'Keep it until we arrive at your door,' he quietly advised, sending a pointed glance at the cab driver. 'One can only imagine what the champagne has done to the fabric of your dress by now.'

She went pale, remembering that awful moment when she'd caught the cab driver's gaze fixed on her breasts, so transparently etched against her sodden dress.

'Thank you,' she whispered, clutching the jacket back around her.

He said nothing, opening the taxi door and stepping out, then turning to help her join him before he bent to pass some money through the driver's open window. Annie supposed that she should offer to pay the fare, but somehow this man gave the impression that he would not appreciate such egalitarian gestures. There was an air of the old-fashioned autocrat about him—an indomitable pride in the set of those wide shoulders flexing beneath the white dress shirt as he straightened and turned back to face her.

She shuddered, feeling oddly as though something or someone had just walked over her grave.

'Y-you should have held the taxi,' she murmured stiffly as the black cab rumbled off down the street, belching out pungent diesel fumes as it went.

If he picked up on her unspoken warning—that if he was standing in the belief that she was going to invite him into her home then he was mistaken—he did not show it, merely shrugging those big shoulders dismissively as he turned towards her black-painted front door.

'Your key?' he prompted.

Disconcerted by his calm indifference to any hint she had given him, she decided grimly not to argue, lowering her pale head to watch her fingers fumble nervously with the tiny catch on her soft gold leather evening bag to get at the key. The quicker she got the door open, the sooner she could get rid of him, she decided, wondering crossly what the heck was the matter with her. She didn't usually feel like this.

She didn't usually get herself into crazy situations like this one either. She was very careful not to do so normally.

Normal. What was normal about any of this?

Refusing to allow her fingers to tremble, she fitted the key into the lock, pushed open the door, then forced herself back around to face him. 'Thank you,' she said firmly, 'for bringing me home. And—' she allowed him a small, dry smile '—for saving my embarrassment.'

'Think nothing of it.' He sent her a little bow that was pure, old-fashioned gallantry and befitted somehow this tall dark man who reminded her so much of a throwback from another age. South American, maybe? she wondered curiously, then shuddered, not wanting him to be. She had a strange, unexplainable suspicion that it would actually hurt her to find that he might be the same nationality as Alvarez.

If he was aware of her curiosity he did not offer to relieve it. Instead, and with another one of those bows, he held his hand out towards her as though he were going to grab hold and push her into the house.

Defensively she took a big step back, bringing herself hard up against the white-painted stone wall behind her, and almost choking on an uplift of clamouring fear.

'My jacket,' he reminded her softly.

Oh, God. Annie closed her eyes, angry with herself because she knew that she was behaving like an idiot and really had no reason for it. He had, as he had pointed out, shown her exemplary behaviour over the whole messy incident!

Except for those kisses, she reminded herself tensely. Those kisses had not been exemplary at all.

Lips pressed tightly together over her clenched teeth, she slipped off the jacket and handed it to him. 'Thank you,' she murmured without looking at him.

'My pleasure,' he drawled, his long fingers sliding delicately over hers as he took the jacket from her. Her own began to tingle, fine, sharp showers of sensation skittering across the surface of her skin to make her tremble as she whipped her arm across her body in an effort to hide herself from those terribly disturbing eyes.

Casually he hooked a finger through the loop and draped the jacket over his shoulder, his lazy stance showing no signs that he was going to go away.

Annie waited, praying fiercely that he was not standing here expecting her to invite him in. No man other than Todd had ever stepped a single foot inside her home.

And only Todd had done so because he had proved time and time again that she could trust him with her very life.

She thought of this house as her sanctuary—the only place where she felt she could relax and truly be herself. She didn't want to give way to the compelling urge he seemed to be silently pressing on her to break that rule and invite him to enter.

Panic began to bubble up from the anxious pit of her stomach—panic at the man's indomitable refusal to be brushed off by her, and panic at the knowledge that if he kept this small, silent battle up she was going to be the one to give in.

Then he touched her.

And, good grief, everything vital inside her went haywire—muscles, nerves, senses, heart, all clamouring out of control as his hand cupped gently at her chin, lifted it, forcing her wary blue gaze to meet the probing expression in his.

He didn't say anything, but a frown marred that high, satin-smooth brow as though he was reassessing—again—and was still not sure what he was seeing when he looked at the infamous Annie Lacey.

'Beautiful,' he murmured almost to himself, then bent suddenly, blocking out the dim lamplight as his mouth swooped down to press a soft, light kiss to her trembling mouth. 'More than beautiful,' he extended as he straightened again. 'Dangerous.' Then he said, 'Goodnight, Miss Lacey,' and simply turned and walked away, leaving her standing there staring at his long, loose, easy stride with his jacket thrown over one broad shoulder while that shocking pelt of raven hair rested comfortably along his straight spine.

And she felt strangely at odds with herself—as though she had just let go of something potentially very important to her and had no way of snatching it back.

CHAPTER THREE

IT WAS crazy, she told herself later as she pulled a smooth satin robe over her freshly showered body.

It had been a crazy night with a crazy end that had left her with this crazy sense of deep disappointment that she couldn't seem to shake off.

What's the matter with you? she asked herself impatiently. You should be feeling relieved, not disappointed that he didn't take advantage of a situation most men would have leapt at if they'd found Annie Lacey beholden to them for something!

Or maybe, she then found herself thinking, it was *because* she was the notorious Annie Lacey that he had not taken advantage. Perhaps he was the kind of man who did not involve himself with the Annie Laceys of this world.

Perhaps, for once, your reputation has worked against you.

What?

No.

'That's sick thinking, Annie,' she muttered to herself.

And anyway, you cannot be feeling annoyed about a lost opportunity you had no intention of taking up yourself!

Remember Luis Alvarez, she told herself grimly. Remembering him was enough to put any woman off all those dark Latin types for good!

With that levelling reminder, she tightened her robe's belt around her waist and flounced out of the bedroom, aware that there was more than a little defiance in the way she slammed the door shut on the thoughts she had left on the other side.

Her house was not big, really nothing more than an old-fashioned terraced cottage renovated to modern-day standards. The upper floor housed her one bedroom, which had been carefully fitted to utilise minimum space for maximum storage, and a rather decadent bathroom, with its spa bath and pulse-action shower that could massage the aches out of the worst day's modelling. The stairway dropped directly into her small sitting room-cum-dining room, where the clever use of lighting and pastel shades made it a pleasure to her eye each time she entered.

The kitchen was a super-efficient blend of modern appliances and limed oak. Annie padded across the cool ceramic floor to fill the kettle for a cup of good, strong tea.

The best panacea to cure all ills, she told herself bracingly. Even the ills of a silly woman in conflict with no one but herself!

Crazy. Crazy, crazy, she sighed to herself as she leant against a unit to gaze out on the dark night while she waited for the kettle to boil.

Most of her life had been lived in busy high profile. Her ability to act and her photogenic looks had been picked up on and used from a very early age. While Aunt Claire had been alive she had been buffered from most of the flak that went with a well-known face by a woman who had been fiercely protective of Annie's privacy. But after her aunt had died and with what came afterwards Annie had suddenly found herself the constant cynosure of all eyes.

Which was why she loved her little house so much. She loved the sense of well-being and security that it always filled her with to be shut alone inside it. It was here and only here that she felt able to relax enough to drop her guard and be herself—though, she then thought, she was not really sure she knew who or what that person was, having never really been given the time or chance to find out.

Was it that sombre-faced person she could see staring back at her in the darkened reflection of the kitchen window? she wondered. She hoped not. Those eyes looked just a little too lost and lonely for her peace of mind, and her mouth had a vulnerable tilt to it that unsettled her slightly because she did not consider herself vulnerable to anything much—except contempt, she conceded. Others' contempt of her could still cut and cut deeply.

As could rejection, she added. Or—to be more precise—cold rejection, usually administered by women who felt threatened by her, but sometimes by men. Men of that stranger's calibre. Cool, self-possessed, autocratic men who—

She pulled herself up short, a frown marring the smooth brow she could see in the window. Now why had her mind skipped back to him again? He had not held her in contempt—or if he had he had not shown it. Nor had he rejected her—not in the ice-cold way she'd been musing about just then.

He was a stranger—just a mere, passing stranger who had helped her out of an embarrassing spot then quietly gone on his way, that was all.

The trouble with you, Annie Lacey, she told herself grimly, is that you've become so damned cynical about the opposite sex that you actually expect every one of them to take advantage of you whenever they possibly can!

And could it be that you're feeling just a teeny bit miffed because he did *not* take advantage of the situation?

I wish...

And just what do you wish? that more sensible side
of her brain derided. For a nice, ordinary man to come
along to sweep you off your dainty feet and take you
away from all of this? Two things wrong with that wish,
Annie. One—you made this particular bed you are now
lying so uncomfortably on. And two—that man was no
ordinary man. He was strong, dark and excitingly
mysterious.

And you fancied him like hell, she finally admitted.
But he obviously did not fancy you!

And that's what you're feeling so miffed about!

She grimaced at that, and was glad that the kettle decided to boil at that moment so that she could switch
her thoughts to other things.

She was just pouring tea into her cup when the tele-
phone began to ring.

Todd, she decided. It had to be. He would be ringing
up to find out just what had happened to her, and a
rueful smile was curving her mouth as she took her cup
of tea with her into her sitting room and dropped into
the corner of a soft-cushioned sofa before lifting the receiver to her ear.

'What the hell happened to you?' It was Todd,
sounding angry and anxious all at the same time, God
bless him. 'One minute you were off to the loo, the next
I'm being informed that you were seen in a mad,
passionate clinch with some guy, then disappearing out
of the door with him! Who the hell is he? And what the
hell were you doing just walking out on me like that?'

She shifted uncomfortably, taking her time curling her
bare toes beneath her while she tried to decide how to
answer all of that. There was no way she was going to
admit the truth, that was for sure. it was bad enough
knowing what a fool she'd been, getting into a taxi with
a complete stranger, but telling Todd of all people that
not only had she done exactly that but she'd also let the

stranger kiss her in front of half of London's best would make him think that she'd gone temporarily insane!

Crazy. The whole thing was crazy.

'Oh, just an old friend from way back,' she heard herself say lightly. 'And we weren't kissing,' she lied. 'We were plotting because some stupid fool had spilled a full glass of champagne down my front, and you don't need much imagination to know what that must have done to my dress.'

'God, yes!' he gasped, obviously not lacking the imagination needed to guess what the skimpy silk would have looked like wet. 'Are you all right? Why didn't you come and get me? Is he still there with you now?'

Annie had to smile at the quick-fired set of questions. 'I'm fine,' she replied. 'I didn't come and get you because quite frankly, darling, I was not in a fit state to go anywhere but straight home. And no, he is not still here.'

'You said an old friend,' he murmured thoughtfully. 'I didn't know you had any male friends but me.'

'Well, there's conceit for you,' she drawled, thinking, He's right, I don't. And she felt suddenly very empty inside.

'Who?' Todd demanded. 'What's his name?'

'No one you know,' she dismissed, realising with a start that she hadn't even bothered to ask his name!

Crazy. You really are going crazy, Annie!

'A male model,' she said, forcing her mind back to Todd's question. 'I met him on that promo I did for Cable last year. Who told you I was kissing him?' she demanded with commendable affront, to throw him off the track.

There was a short pause before his deriding, 'Guess,' came down the line at her.

'Susie,' she sighed. She should have known.

'She took great delight in telling me how she'd seen you lost in a heated clinch with another man before you walked off and left me,' he related grimly. 'Then had the bloody gall to suggest I see her home instead!'

'To which you replied?' she prompted.

'Guess again, darling,' he drawled. 'I'm still here at this wretched mêlée if that gives you a clue.'

Yes, it gave her a big clue, and Annie's heart ached for him.

'If she thought she could walk up to me and start slandering you in one breath then expect me to fall back into her arms in the next then she soon learned otherwise,' he went on tightly. 'She eventually left with that guy from the Rouez Sands Group.'

'And made sure you saw her leave with him, of course.'

'Oh, yes,' he sighed.

'You OK?' she asked him gently.

'No,' he said. 'But I'll live.'

Annie smothered a sigh, wishing that she could ease the pain she knew he was suffering right now. But only Susie could do that, and the foolish woman was too jealous of Annie to see that by blackening Annie to Todd she was only making things worse for herself.

In all fairness Annie didn't completely blame Susie for being suspicious about their relationship. It did look suspicious to anyone looking in on it. But even though she'd urged Todd often enough to tell Susie the truth he'd refused, going all stiff and adamant in a way that told her that Susie's suspicions offended his pride. 'It cuts both ways,' was all he ever said. 'If she can't trust my word that there is nothing intimate between you and me, then why should I trust her with the full truth about us?'

Stalemate, and likely to stay that way while both of them remained so pig-headed about it all.

'Give me a call soon,' he murmured as a conclusion to the conversation, then added as an afterthought, 'But not during the rest of this week, because I'll be in Madrid trying to whip up that extra injection of cash I need to secure *Cliché* Europe's safe launch.'

Annie frowned, having forgotten all about that. Todd had told her about it only this evening—the surprising and worrying fact that he was taking a big risk publishing a new glossy in the present economic climate. 'The trouble is,' he'd explained ruefully, 'I stagnate if I don't and stand to lose everything if I do.'

'What I need,' he murmured thoughtfully now, 'is something really exclusive to front the first issue— something that will guarantee sales and therefore appeal to my backers. I just haven't come up with what that exclusive something is yet.'

'You will,' she stated, with soft confidence in his ability. 'And if all else fails I could always pose nude,' she suggested. 'That'll be a world first and guarantee you a complete sell-out.'

'You'd do it too, wouldn't you?' he murmured curiously, hearing the note of seriousness threading through her lighter tone.

'For you?' she said. 'I would sell my very soul for you, my darling, and that's the truth. But I would much rather not,' she then added. 'So try to come up with something less—sensational for me, will you?' she pleaded.

'I promise,' he laughed. 'Not that the idea of you posing nude does not appeal,' he teased. 'But I think I should be able to come up with something more—subtle. So take care, and be good while I'm away.'

When am I ever anything else? Annie thought as she replaced the receiver and grimaced at the dark sense of dissatisfaction that began niggling at her nerves.

And all because a stranger managed to get beneath that protective skin you wear? she mocked herself.

'Goodness me, Annie,' she muttered aloud, and then thought, You must be feeling starved of affection to have one small incident affect you as much as you're allowing this to do.

Bed, she decided. Bed before you become even more maudlin than you already are!

But she didn't sleep well, her dreams seeming haunted by a tall dark figure who kept insisting on kissing her, his warm mouth constantly closing over her own every time she tried to speak! But, worse than that, she didn't try to fight him but always, always welcomed him— helplessly, eagerly! Then she ended up waking in a breathless state of shock at her own wanton imagination.

It was terrible. She was ashamed of herself! 'Sex-starved, that's what you are,' she muttered, and gave her pillow an angry thump before settling down to experience the self-same dream all over again!

Consequently she was not in a very good frame of mind when her phone began ringing at what felt like the break of dawn that morning.

Grumbling incoherently to herself, she tried to ignore it at first, stuffing her head beneath her pillow and pretending the noise was not there. But it didn't stop, and after a while she sighed, sat up, rubbed at her gritty eyes then reached out with a lazy hand to lift the receiver.

'Annie!' Lissa's excited voice hit her eardrums like the clash from a hundred cymbals. 'Get our neat botty out of that bed! *Cliché*'s got its launch. And we have one hell of a panic on!'

A panic. She would call it more than a panic, Annie decided grumpily as she dragged herself to the transit lounge at Barbados's Grantley Adams airport over twelve hours later.

'But I'm due in Paris on Tuesday!' she'd exclaimed in protest when Lissa had finished giving her the hurried details of Todd's great coup.

'All changed, darling,' her agent had said. 'Everything cancelled for the next two weeks in favour of this.'

'This' being Todd's brainwave—which had apparently hit him after he had been talking to her on the phone last night.

Or—to be more precise—someone else had hit him with it.

The great and glorious Adamas, no less.

And, even despite not wanting to be, Annie was impressed.

Adamas jewellery was the most expensive anyone could buy. The man who worked under that trade name was a legend because he designed and produced every single breathtakingly exquisite piece himself, using only the finest stones and setting them in precious metal. All the world's richest women clamoured to possess them.

He was a genius in his field. His last collection had taken five years to put together, and had sold out in five minutes. That must have been—Annie frowned, trying to remember—four years ago at least.

And late last night, it seemed, Todd had found himself talking to none other than Adamas himself! He hadn't known, of course, whom he was sharing a nightcap with. Hardly anyone alive on this earth knew who the real Adamas actually was, because the man was some kind of eccentric recluse!

But, according to Lissa, during this chat over a drink Todd's journalistic mind must have been alerted by something Adamas had said, and he'd begun to suspect just whom he was drinking with. So he had gone for it—asked the man outright—and, lo and behold, found out that he was right!

One thing had led to another, and a few drinks later Todd had discovered that the guy had just completed his latest collection. And that had been when his brainstorm had hit. A blind shot, he'd called it. He'd suggested what a coup it would be if *Cliché* launched with Annie Lacey wearing the latest Adamas collection. And to his surprise the great man had agreed!

And that, neatly put, was why Annie had just spent the last twelve hours travelling.

Adamas had agreed, but only on his own strict terms—one being that the whole thing had to take place immediately or not at all, another that he chose the location and—something insisted on because of the priceless value of the subject matter in hand—that the whole thing must be carried out in the utmost secrecy!

Which was also why she was now stuck in transit, waiting to find out what the rest of her travel arrangements were. Lissa had only been privy to Annie's travel plan this far. The rest was to be revealed.

But that would not be before she'd had a chance to change out of the faded jeans and baggy old sweatshirt that had been part of her disguise along with a sixties floppy velvet hat into which she'd had her hair stuffed for the last twelve hours to comply with his demand for secrecy, she decided grimly.

She was hot, she was tired, and she felt grubby. And, grabbing her flight bag, she made her way to the ladies' room, deciding that any further travelling could wait until she felt more comfortable.

Half an hour later, and dressed more appropriately for the Caribbean in a soft white Indian cotton skirt and matching blouse, with her hair scooped into a high topknot, she was being ushered out into the burning sun and across the tarmac towards a twin engined, eight-seater aeroplane which was to take her to Union Island, the gateway to the Grenadines, or so she'd been informed by the attendant who'd come to collect her.

An hour after that she found herself standing in the shimmering heat of her third airport of the day, where a beautiful young woman with perfect brown skin and a gentle smile was trying to usher her towards a waiting helicopter!

'But where am I supposed to be going to?' she demanded irritably, growing tired of all this cloak-and-dagger stuff.

'To one of our beautiful smaller islands, privately leased from our government by your host,' the young woman informed her smoothly, and strode off in the wake of Annie's luggage, which was being carried by an airport lackey.

'Host,' she muttered tetchily. Did anyone know the actual name of the great Adamas? Or did his desire for privacy mean that even his name was a carefully guarded secret?

Her luggage had been stowed by the time she reached the helicopter, its lethal blades already rotating impatiently. She was instructed to duck her head a little as she ran beneath them, then was helped to clamber in beside the pilot.

With a smile and a gesture of farewell the young woman closed the door, and the sudden change from deafening noise to near silence was a shock. Annie straightened in her seat, smoothed down the soft folds of her skirt, blinked a couple of times in an effort to clear her bewildered head, then turned to look at the pilot.

And almost fainted in surprise.

Long black hair, tied back at the tanned nape by a thin black strip of ribbon, lean dark face with green eyes smiling sardonically at her.

It was her rescuer from the night before.

And the man she had let seduce her all night long in her dreams.

'You!' she gasped, feeling an upsurge of guilty heat burn her insides when her eyes automatically dropped to his shockingly familiar mouth.

'Good afternoon, Miss Lacey,' he drawled, enjoying the reaction he was having on her.

'But—what are you doing here?'

'Why, I live here,' he smoothly replied, and touched something that sent a burst of power into the engines. 'Please fasten yourself in; we are about to take off.'

'But...' She couldn't move for the shock of it. 'You're a helicopter pilot?' she choked out eventually.

'Among other things.' He smiled, humour leaping to that magnetically attractive mouth at what, Annie realised almost as soon as she'd said it, was about the most stupid thing she had ever said. 'Your belt,' he prompted. 'We will talk later.'

Then he was flicking the headset he had resting around his neck up over his ears and dismissing her as he turned his attention to the task in hand, leaving her to fumble numbly with her belt while he spoke smoothly to air-traffic control. Then, without warning, they were up in the air.

Annie gasped at the unexpectedness of it, staring with wide eyes as the ground simply dropped away beneath them. Her heart leapt into her mouth, her lungs refused to function, and, of course, the slight numbing effect of jet lag was not helping her discern what the heck was going on here.

They paused, hovering like a hawk about to swoop, then shot forwards in a way that threw her back into her seat. He glanced at her sharply, then away again, a small smile playing about his lips which seemed to err more towards satisfaction than anything else.

Then suddenly she was covering her eyes as they seemed to shoot directly towards the bright orange ball of sun hanging low in the sky.

Something dropped on her lap. Peering down, she saw a pair of gold-rimmed sunglasses and gratefully pushed them on. Able to see again without suffering for it, she turned to look curiously at him.

He too had donned a pair of sunglasses; gold-rimmed like her own pair, they sat neatly across the bridge of his long, thin nose, seeming to add a certain pizzazz to an already rivetingly attractive face.

Last time she'd seen him he had been standing at her front door wearing a severely conventional black dinner suit and bow-tie. He had seemed alarmingly daunting to her fanciful mind then.

Now those same sparks of alarm came back to worry her, darting across her skin, because here in this contraption, with the full blast of the Caribbean sun shining on his face, he had taken on a far more dangerously appealing appearance. His skin looked richer, his features more keenly etched. The thin cream shirt he was wearing was tucked into the pleated waist of a pair of wheat-coloured linen slacks, offering a more casual view of him that made her want to back off even while she was drawn towards it.

'Why are you here?' she asked as her nerves began to steady. 'Or—' she then clarified that '—why am I here with you?'

'You do not know?' He flicked her a glance before returning his attention to what he was doing, but the look had been enough to make her stupid mind click into action, and she sat there staring at him in utter disbelief.

'You—are Adamas?' she gasped.

He didn't answer—didn't need to. It was written in that small smile that touched briefly at the corner of his mouth. 'We are going to my island,' he informed her smoothly instead. 'It sits just beyond the main string of islands, lapped by the Caribbean on one side and the Atlantic on the other...'

Annie was barely listening; she was still staring unblinkingly at him, trying to fit her impression of what the Adamas man should look like to the one he actually was!

An eccentric recluse? This—Adonis of a man with more muscle than fat and an air about him that still made her think more of the Spanish Inquisition than an artistic genius. Blinking, she found herself staring at his hands—long hands, strong hands with the signs of manual labour scored into the supple palms, long fingers, blunt-ended, with neatly shorn nails. The hands of a man who worked fine metal into those intricate designs that she had been privileged to glimpse once around the neck of a very wealthy woman?

'I don't believe it,' she muttered, more to herself than to him.

But he shrugged carelessly, as if her opinion did not bother him. 'I am what I am, Miss Lacey,' he drawled indifferently. Then almost too casually he went on, 'As you are what you undoubtedly are.'

An insult—Annie didn't even try to mistake it for anything but what it was. But before she could challenge him about it again they veered sharply to one side, sending her heart leaping into her mouth again when she found herself staring sideways out of the helicopter onto a half-moon stretch of glistening silver sand.

'My home,' he announced. 'Or one of them,' he then added coolly. 'The island is a quarter of a mile wide and half a mile long. It has a shape like a hooked nose which is where it gets its name—Hook-nose Island. My villa sits in the hook—see?'

Dipping the helicopter, he swooped down towards the island, bringing the two-storey white plantation-style house swinging dizzyingly up towards them. Then, before she had time to catch her breath at that little bit of showmanship, he levelled the helicopter off and hovered so that she could focus on the palm-tree-lined lawns that swept down from the house to the silver beach she had seen first.

'Hook-nose Bay is a bathers' paradise,' he said. 'The natural curve of the land itself and the coral reef at the bay's mouth protect it from the worst of the weather and any unwelcome aquatic visitors with sharp teeth.'

'Sharks?' she asked nervously.

He nodded. 'These islands are famous for their resident Nurse Sharks. But it is safe to bathe there in the bay—though the rest of the island is not so safe,' he warned. 'Strong currents and sometimes angry seas can make bathing on any of the other little coves you see quite dangerous. Especially on the Atlantic side.'

As he turned them neatly to face in the opposite direction Annie gazed curiously down to where a thick tropical wood clustered around a hump in the centre of the island, at the bottom of which the house nestled against its lushly carpeted slope. On the other side of the hill sheer drops of craggy rock fell abruptly downwards to jagged inlets where the Atlantic tossed itself against them in foaming white crests.

This side of the little island was a stark contrast to the other softer, more gentle side that the house faced. It would be an unlucky sailor who came upon this island from that direction, she noted with a small shudder.

Then she gasped as they began to drop like a stone towards the ground. They landed gently, though, her sigh of relief bringing a mocking look from the man beside her before he turned his attention to shutting down the engine and going through some kind of mental check-list before he opened his door and jumped out.

He came around to help her, having to stoop low be-neath the slowing blades and warning her to do the same as his hands circled her slender waist to assist her. Then they were running free, both bent almost double, Annie with a hand covering her eyes to stop the whirls of dust from blowing into them.

Pulling to a halt about ten yards away from the heli-copter, he turned to watch as she dusted down her clothes with her hands. They'd landed on a natural plateau of rock not far away from the house. But, sand being sand, it had found its way up here, blown probably by the trade winds that acted like natural air-conditioning to most of these islands.

'Come,' he said when she'd concluded her tidy-up by brushing light fingertips over her hair and cheeks. 'I will bring your luggage later. But now you must be in dire need of a drink.'

She was and didn't demur, following him across a neatly kept lawn and up the few steps which took them into the lower veranda's shade.

The two solid wood front doors stood open in welcome. He led the way into a deliciously cool entrance hall, where Annie paused to catch her breath and study with still slightly bewildered eyes the blatant luxury of Aubusson thrown down on top of richly polished wood.

For a mere hallway it was huge—as big as any other room in a house of this size. 'Grand' was the word that slid into her mind. Old masters with a nautical theme hung in heavy gold frames on plain, white-painted walls and a great staircase swept up from its central location to a galleried landing that seemed to form a circle around the whole upper floor.

A woman appeared from the back of the house. Short, thin and wiry, with greying hair swept away from a severe face, she was wearing all black. She greeted her employer with some words in what Annie half-recognised as Spanish, to which he replied in the same language, his voice seeming to grow more liquid, more sensually disturbing to Annie's agitated mind.

'Margarita,' he informed Annie, watching as the two women exchanged shy, slightly stiff smiles. 'Between them, she and her husband Pedro take care of everything here. If you will please come this way—' he held out an arm in invitation '—Margarita will bring us some refreshment.'

As the woman bustled off towards the back of the house Annie followed her host across the hall and into a large, bright, sunny room with full-length French-style windows standing open to the gentle sea breeze.

Momentarily diverted, she moved over to look at the view, and stood transfixed by what she saw. Before her lay a dramatic mix of lush green lawns rolling down towards a crescent of silver sand, followed by the pale aquamarine shades of shallow waters deepening to rich gentian-blue. Several beautiful flame-trees with their branches laden with vivid red blooms were scattered around the grounds. The sun was hanging low—a deep golden globe shimmering in a melting turquoise sky.

And when she heard movement behind her she turned an enraptured smile to the man she found propped up against the closed door, mockery and arrogance in every line of his body as he stood there with one neat ankle crossed over the other, arms folded across his big chest.

'Well, well,' he drawled. 'So the notorious Miss Lacey can still experience a childlike enchantment at something beautiful and unspoiled. Who would have thought it?'

Annie went still, her smile dying as she was suddenly assailed by a cold, dark sense of menace, his lazy masculine stance, his insolent expression and his deriding words all helping to remind her of something that she should have never let herself forget. Men were the enemy. And this particular man was no different.

'Who are you?' she demanded quietly.

'Who am I?' he repeated, the mockery hard and spiked. 'Why, I am Adamas,' he informed her lazily. 'Loosely translated, it means diamond-hard—impenetrable. But in this case we shall call me a—rock,' he decided. 'A rock on which you, Annie Lacey, have just been neatly marooned.'

CHAPTER FOUR

'Marooned.' Annie frowned at him, trying to decide whether he was just attempting a very poor joke. But his face held no hint of humour, only a smile that sent the blood running cold through her veins.

Marooned, she repeated silently and slowly to herself. Abandoned. Isolated without resources. He had used the word quite deliberately.

It hit her then that this was no simple commission in which the great Adamas employed the notorious Annie Lacey to promote his priceless gems. She had been brought here under false pretences—brought here and isolated from the rest of the world by this man for some specific purpose of his own.

A sick sense of *déjà vu* washed over her, filling her eyes with unmistakable horror as Luis Alvarez's hot face loomed up in her mind, and for a moment—a small moment—she lost control, face paling, breasts heaving, eyes haunted as they glanced around for somewhere to run.

'Perfect,' he drawled, making her blink at the soft-voiced sensuality that he managed to thread into the one simple word. 'That look of maidenly panic must have taken hours of practice in front of your mirror to cultivate. Allow that gorgeous mouth to quiver just a little,' he suggested, 'and you will be well on the way to convincing me that the well-seasoned vamp is actually a terrified virgin.'

Margarita used that moment to knock on the door. He moved smoothly, loose-limbed and lazily controlled, to open the door and stand aside while his shyly smiling servant wheeled in a trolley laid out with coffee things and some daintily prepared sandwiches.

Annie watched, unable to so much as move a muscle as the other woman murmured in Spanish to her employer and he answered in deep casual replies. The trolley was wheeled over to stand beside a low table between two big, soft-cushioned sofas of a pale coral-pink. Then Margarita was leaving again, murmuring what must have been her thanks to her employer for holding the door for her.

'Who are you really?' Annie demanded once they were alone. 'And will you kindly explain what this—stupid charade is all about?'

'I am who I said I am,' he replied with infuriating blandness. 'I am Adamas. I told you no lies, Miss Lacey.' Moving gracefully, he went over to the trolley then turned a questioning look at her. 'Tea—coffee?' he asked. 'Margarita has prepared both.'

Impatiently Annie shook her head. She wanted nothing in this house until she got some answers. Nothing. 'Is that supposed to make sense to me?' she snapped out impatiently.

'No,' he conceded. 'But then—I never meant to.' A brief smile touched his mouth before he turned his attention to pouring himself a cup of dark, rich coffee. The aroma drifted across the room to torment Annie's parched mouth, forcing her to swallow drily, but other than that she ignored the temptation to change her mind. 'Won't you at least sit down?' he offered politely.

Again she shook her head—for the same reason. 'I just want you to tell me what is going on,' she insisted.

He studied her for a moment, those strange green eyes glinting thoughtfully at her from between glossy black lashes, as if he was considering forcing her to sit and drink.

Whatever, the look had the effect of pushing up her chin, her blue eyes challenging him just to try it and see what he got!

Though what he would get if he did decide to force her physically, she wasn't sure. She was tall, but this man seemed to fill the whole room with his threatening presence. And she couldn't help quailing deep down inside because she knew that if he did call her bluff she would have no choice but to do exactly what he wanted her to do.

And it is that, Annie, she told herself grimly, which keeps you standing as far away from him as you can get! He reminds you of Luis Alvarez—the same height, the same colouring, the same arrogance that made men like them believe that they could say, be and do anything they liked! And if he was Adamas then he also possessed the same money and power in society to have anything nasty about himself that he would not wish the world to hear covered up.

Like the abduction of unwilling females.

She shuddered, unable to control herself. She should have known from the moment she laid eyes on him last night—had known! Her well-tuned instincts had sent out warning signals straight away! But she had let his easy manner lull her into a false sense of security. And, dammit, she'd liked him! Actually allowed herself to like him for the way he had behaved!

She had never been able to say that for Luis, she remembered bitterly. Luis Alvarez had turned her stomach from the moment she'd found herself alone with him. But then, Luis Alvarez had been at least ten years older than this man, his good looks spoiled by ten years' more cynicism and dissolution.

This man did not turn her stomach in that same way, she realised worriedly. And maybe that was one of the reasons why he frightened her perhaps more than Alvarez had ever done. He frightened her because she was reluctantly attracted to him. His calculating study of her frightened her. His softly spoken words that held so many hidden messages frightened her. But, above all, the actual air she was breathing was frightening her— simply because it was filled with the appealing scent of him.

Did he know it? she wondered anxiously. Could he tell what kind of effect he was having on her? His eyes were burning over her—burning in a way that told her that, whatever else was going on here, he too liked what he saw.

The air thickened, became impossible to breathe as the silence between them grew hot and heavy. Then, without warning, he looked down and away.

It was like having something vital taken from her, and Annie had to measure carefully the air she dragged into her suddenly gasping lungs in case she should hyperventilate.

'OK,' he conceded coolly. 'We talk.'

He brought those green eyes to hers again, and there was something overwhelmingly proud in the way his chin lifted along with the eyes.

'My name,' he announced, 'is César DeSanquez. Adamas is merely a name under which I trade...'

DeSanquez, DeSanquez, Annie was thinking frowningly. The name rang a rather cold bell inside her head. It was a name that evoked an image of great wealth and power—an image wrapped in oil and gold and diamonds and—

'I am American-Venezuelan by birth, but my roots are firmly planted in my Venezuelan links.'

And it hit. It hit with a sickening sense of understanding that made her sway where she stood.

'Ah,' he murmured. 'I see you are beginning to catch on. Yes, Miss Lacey,' he softly confirmed, 'Cristina

Alvarez is my sister. And you made the quick connection, I must assume, because your—affair with my brother-in-law took place in the DeSanquez apartment. The media made quite a meal out of these—juicy facts, did they not? In fact, their attention to detail was quite remarkably concise—the way they told of Annie Lacey lying with her lover in one bed while her lover's wife lay asleep in another bedroom of her brother's apartment. My apartment, Miss Lacey,' he enunciated thinly. 'My bed!'

Annie sank tremulously into a nearby chair, his anger, his contempt and his disgust breaking over her in cold, sickening waves while she fought with her own sense of anger and disgust—disgust for a single night in her life that would always, it seemed, come back to haunt her for as long as she lived.

She had gone to that apartment by invitation, to a party being held by a man called DeSanquez—a wealthy young Venezuelan who had expressed a desire to meet the sweet Angel Lacey, as everyone had called her then. She never had actually met the Venezuelan, she remembered now in surprise, because she hadn't given him a thought after meeting Alvarez instead.

Alvarez. She shuddered.

'Quite,' he observed. 'I acknowledge your horror. It was a revolting time for all of us. Not least my sister,' he pointed out. 'Having to walk into my bedroom and find you in my bed, not with me—it would not have mattered if it had been me,' he drawled. 'But to find you with her own husband was a terrible shock. It effectively ruined her marriage and ultimately almost ruined her life.

'For this alone,' he explained with a hateful coolness, 'I feel perfectly justified in demanding retribution from you—and indeed would have done so at the time this all happened if my sister had not begged me to let it be.

So, for Cristina's sake, and for Cristina's alone,' he made absolutely clear, 'I went against my personal desire to strangle the unscrupulous life out of you right there and then. But—that is not the end of it.'

Turning, he moved to place his coffee-cup on the top of the white marble fireplace then rested his arm alongside it. Every move he made, every unconscious gesture was so incredibly graceful that even in the middle of all of this Annie found herself drawn by him.

'I mentioned my dual nationality for a good reason,' he continued, his tone—as it had been throughout—utterly devoid of emotion. 'For although my father was Venezuelan my mother was, in actual fact, American. Now,' he asserted, as though relaying a mildly interesting piece of history, 'her name before she married my father was Frazer— Ah, I see you are quick. Yes.' He smiled thinly as Annie licked her suddenly dry lips. 'Susie is my cousin. Quite a coincidence, is it not, that you should happen to be the woman trying to ruin her life just as carelessly as you ruined my sister Cristina's?'

Annie closed her eyes, shutting out the crucifying blandness of his expression as he watched her. She had been wrong before when she'd believed him to be of the same ilk as Luis. He was in actual fact very different, if only because Luis had cared only for his own rotten neck while this man seemed to hold himself personally responsible for the necks of others.

Which in turn made him very dangerous because, in deciding to make himself an avenger, it was obvious that he was quite prepared to endanger his own neck to get retribution for those he loved. Blindly loved, she added heavily to herself. And she suddenly felt very, very sorry for him.

To each his Achilles heel, she mused starkly, opening her eyes to show him a perfectly cool expression. Luis Alvarez's Achilles heel had been his inflated ego, and the arrogant belief that power and money could buy for his bed any woman he'd desired. Cristina's had been her blindness to what her husband actually was. And Susie's was her need to have everything her selfish heart desired.

This man's was his fierce love for his family.

She then found herself wondering what her own Achilles heel was. She didn't know, but she had a horrible feeling that in this man's hands she was going to find out.

'You have nothing to say?' Her calmness was irritating him; she could see the annoyance begin to glint in his strange green eyes.

Green. 'No,' she answered. 'Not a single thing.' And another realisation hit her squarely in the face. Susie had green eyes—the same green eyes. Which seemed to tie the whole situation off neatly for her. She didn't have a cat-in-hell's chance of making this man with those eyes see anything from her point of view, so she wasn't even going to try. 'Perhaps you would, therefore, like to continue?' she invited, knowing with certainty that he had not offered her all of this information just for the fun of it.

His sudden burst of angry movement at her seeming indifference took her by surprise, because he had been so purposefully controlled up until then. His hand flicked down from the mantel, his body straightening tautly. 'Has nothing I have said managed to reach you?' he demanded harshly.

'It would seem not,' she said. 'All I've heard until now is a potted description of your family tree. Very interesting, I'm sure,' she drawled, 'but nothing for me to get fired up about.'

He didn't like it. He didn't like the fact that she could maintain a cool façade and even go as far as mocking him.

It served him right, she thought, for his arrogant supposition that he had a right to speak to her like this! If he had taken the trouble to find out about her—really find out instead of restricting his knowledge to pure tabloid gossip and the malicious judgement of his thankless family—then he would have discovered that few people managed to rile Annie Lacey with mere words. Out of sheer necessity she had grown a thick skin around herself to protect her from the cruel thrust of words, and it would take a better man than he to pierce that protective skin.

'When they say you possess none of the finer senses they are right, aren't they?' he muttered. 'Do you feel no hint of compassion for others at all?'

'It would seem not,' she said again, fielding his contempt with blue eyes that gave away nothing of what she was thinking or feeling inside. Then sheer devilment made her cock a golden eyebrow at him. 'Is there any in you?' she challenged right back.

'For you, you mean?' He shook his sleek dark head. 'No, Miss Lacey, I am sorry to inform you that I harbour not an ounce of compassion for you.'

'Then you have no right to expect more from me than you are willing to give yourself,' she said, and got up, her slender body no less sensuous in movement because it was stiff with control. He couldn't know, of course, that she had been through this kind of character-slaying before, and at far more lethal hands than his, or he would not be trying this tactic out on her.

'Where do you think you are going?' he demanded as she walked towards the door.

'Why, to the one place you obviously expect me to go,' she replied. 'To the devil. But by my route, Mr DeSanquez, I will do it by my own route.'

He moved like lightning, had to to reach the door even before she had a chance to turn the handle. His hand, big and slightly callused, closed around her own. Even with the light clasp he exerted, the hand managed to intimidate her.

'And how do you mean to get there?' he enquired silkily. 'Fly on your broomstick as witches do? Or are you more the snake, Miss Lacey, prepared to slither your way across the ocean to your devil's lair?'

'Funny,' she jeered, having to force herself to retaliate through the stifling breathlessness that she was suddenly experiencing at his closeness. 'But I thought this was the devil's lair?'

'I am merely his servant, Angelica,' he stated grimly. 'Merely his servant.'

There was nothing 'mere' about this man. He was larger than life itself—in size, in presence, in the sheer, physical threat of the man.

'I want to leave here,' she informed him coldly.

'But I've not finished with you yet.' The taunting words were murmured against her cheek, dampening her skin with his warm spicy breath.

'But I have finished with you!' she snapped, turning to anger to cover up the hectic effect his closeness was having on her. 'I demand that you fly me back to Union Island!' She tried to prise his fingers from her other hand. 'Now—before this silly game gets out of hand!'

He responded by snaking a hard arm around her waist and lifting her off the ground. Ignoring the way she twisted and struggled and kicked out with feet made ineffectual by the way he was carrying her, he walked over to the sofa and dropped her unceremoniously into the soft coral-coloured cushions, then came to lean threateningly over her.

'Now listen to me,' he commanded. 'And listen well, for this is no game. I mean business, Miss Lacey—serious business. You are here on my island for one purpose only, and that is to put you right out of circulation. From now on I am going to ensure personally that you form no danger to anyone in my family again!'

He was talking about Susie now, of course, Annie realised. 'And how do you intend to do that?' she asked, blue eyes flashing a scornful challenge at green, absolutely refusing to let him see how very frightened she was. 'By ruining my good reputation when everyone knows I don't have one? Or do you have murder in mind, Mr DeSanquez?' she taunted dangerously.

His anger flared at her refusal to take him seriously, his bared teeth flashing bright white in a cruel dark face as he reached for her again. 'Murder is too easy an escape for you, you little she-devil,' he muttered. 'Perhaps this will teach you to have a healthy fear of me!'

She didn't expect it, which was why he caught her so totally off guard when his hard fingers curled tightly on her shoulders and he brought her wrenchingly upwards to meet the punishing force of his mouth.

It lasted only seconds, but it was long enough for her to feel again the hectic sensation of her whole body burning up, as though something totally alien had invaded her.

She didn't move, did not so much as breathe or blink an eyelash in response, yet, as she had been the evening before, she was suddenly and excruciatingly aware of him—aware of his strength, of the power behind the muscles that strained angrily against her, of the subtle, pleasing scent of him, the smooth texture of his tight, tanned skin.

Her mouth was burning, her soft lips throbbing where he pressed them bruisingly back against her tightly clenched teeth. And her breasts—the damning traitors that they were—were responding to the heated pressure of his hard chest, the sensitive tips hardening into tight, tingling sensors of pleasure as they pushed eagerly towards him.

He muttered something in his throat and whipped a hand around the back of her neck so that he could arch her backwards, the other hand coming up between them to let a throbbing nipple push against his palm.

Annie gasped at the shocking insolence of the action, trying to pull away from him. But her gasp gave him entry into her mouth, and the next thing she knew she was being flung into a heady vortex of hot, moist intimacy.

Never—never since Alvarez—had she let a man kiss her like this. The very idea of it had always appalled her. But with this man it was the most achingly sensual experience of her life!

And that appalled her. It appalled her to know that she could be so receptive to a man who held her in such open contempt! And when he eventually lifted his head it was an act of sheer self-preservation that made her stare up at him with apparent indifference to the attack when in actual fact she was slowly and systematically collapsing inside.

'Well, well, well,' she heard herself murmur with an inner horror at her own gall. 'So you too are prepared to use sex to get what you want. And there I was, thinking you way above that kind of thing. How very disappointing.'

He stiffened violently at the taunt, then smiled ruefully when her meaning sank in. 'Ah,' he drawled. 'You are implying that we are similar creatures. But that is not the case,' he denied. 'You see, I do not sleep around—especially with promiscuous bitches who run a high risk of contamination.'

That cut—cut hard and deep. Not that she let him see it, her bruised and trembling mouth taking on a deriding twist as she taunted softly right back, 'Then I think you should tell your body that, because it seems to me that it's quite fancying a bit of contamination right now.' And she let her eyes drop to where the evidence of his own response to the kiss thrust powerfully against Annie's groin.

He dumped her so suddenly that she flailed back into the soft cushions behind her, but she barely noticed because her gaze was fixed incredulously on his hard, angry face.

He'd flushed—he'd actually flushed! She had absolutely thrown him by daring to point out his own sexual response, and elation at managing to get to him made her eyes flash with triumph.

Spinning away from her, he went to pour himself a drink—not coffee this time, but something stronger from a crystal decanter standing on a beautiful mahogany sideboard by the fireplace.

Annie got to her feet, studying him with more curiosity than fear now as that small revelation helped her to diminish the godlike proportions she had been allowing herself to see in him.

How old was he? she found herself wondering curiously. Thirty-one—thirty-two? Not much older, she was certain, though her original impression last night—had it only been last night?—had been of a much older, more mature man.

'Don't you think it's time you told me exactly what it is you do want from me?' she suggested when the silence began to drag between them.

He turned with glass in hand. 'What I want from you is quite simple,' he said, having got his temper back under control, she noted. 'I want you taken right out of Hanson's life, and I intend personally to make sure it happens.'

Todd? She stared at him, amazed that she could have forgotten all about Todd! Even when he'd brought Susie into this Annie had only connected the other girl with their modelling war. Susie's connection with Todd had not even entered her head!

Stupid! she berated herself. How damned stupid can you get? Of course this was all about Todd and Susie, and not just Susie and the *Cliché* contract!

It was like being on a see-saw, she likened heavily. One minute feeling the uplift of her own confidence returning before she crashed down again so abruptly that she was starting to feel dizzy.

'How long have you known Hanson?' he asked her suddenly.

Almost all my life, Annie thought, with a smile that seemed to soften the whole structure of her face. Then she shrugged, slender shoulders shifting inside the white cotton top. 'None of your business,' she said.

He grimaced, as if acknowledging her right to be uncooperative. Yet he tried again—on a slightly different tack. 'But you have been lovers on an off for—what— four years, is it now?'

'No comment.'

He took a sip at his drink, green eyes thoughtful as they ran slowly over her. Annie fixed him with a bland stare; she was determined to give him no help whatsoever.

'You are very beautiful,' he remarked, making her eyelashes flicker in memory of the way he had said that to her the night before. 'Incredibly so for someone who has led such a chequered life. It is no wonder my brother-in-law lost his head over you.'

'Something you are determined not to do,' she reminded him, smiling although the fact that just thinking of Luis Alvarez was enough to turn her stomach.

'And Hanson,' he continued, as if she had not spoken. 'He cannot seem to help himself where you are concerned.'

'Is this conversation supposed to be leading somewhere?' she asked. 'Only, if it is, would you kindly get to the point so I can get out of here? I am tired and would like to get off this island so I can book into a hotel somewhere and get some sleep tonight.'

'Oh, you will get your sleep, Miss Lacey,' he assured her smoothly. 'Plenty of it—in the bed already waiting for you upstairs. You see...' He paused—entirely for effect, Annie suspected. 'As from tonight you became my mistress, and therefore will sleep wherever I sleep.'

'*What*—?' Annie began to laugh. She couldn't help it; the whole thing was getting so ridiculous that she was truly beginning to believe that she must be stuck in some real-as-life nightmare—one of those where nothing made any sense!

'Oh, not in the physical sense of the word,' he inserted coolly into her laughter, 'since we have already established that I have no wish to go where too many men have been before me.'

'Have we?' Her blue eyes mocked him. He lifted his chin and ignored the silent taunt.

'It is, therefore, simple logic to assume that I mean to create the illusion of intimacy—solely for the minds of others.'

'And I'm supposed to meekly go along with all of this, am I?' she murmured with rueful scorn.

Funnily enough, instead of getting angry with her again, he grimaced. 'No,' he conceded. 'Not meekly, I do acknowledge. But I fail to see what you can do about it since this is my island, and the only form of transport off it is in my helicopter. And,' he continued while Annie grimly took all of that in, 'considering I hold the very success of Hanson's launch into Europe in the palm of my hand, I think I can—persuade you to do exactly what I want you to do. If only for Hanson's sake,' he added carefully.

Annie's spine straightened slowly, her attention well and truly fixed now. 'What is that supposed to mean?' she demanded.

'Exactly what it said.' He rid himself of his glass then shoved his hands into the pockets of his lightweight trousers. The action drew her eyes unwillingly downwards to that place where the evidence of his arousal had been so obviously on show.

Not so now. The man was back in control of his body, his stance supremely relaxed. 'As I suppose you must already know, Hanson has overstretched his resources going into Europe,' he went on smoothly. 'He is in dire need of a world exclusive to get his new magazine off the ground. Convincing me to let him publish my new collection is undoubtedly that world exclusive. Using your body to display that collection means he cannot fail. And indeed,' he went on while Annie stood taking it all in, 'I have no wish for him to fail. It would not suit my cousin, you see, for the man she loves to be a failure,' he pointed out. 'But,' he then warned chillingly, 'I am prepared to have him fail if you are not prepared to do exactly what I say.'

The bottom line, Annie recognised as he fell into a meaningful silence. They had just reached the bottom line—as far as any protest from her went anyway. Because from the moment he said he was able to hurt Todd she had been beaten. She would do anything for Todd. Lay down her life for Todd.

Prostitute herself for Todd.

'Tell me exactly what you want me to do,' she said huskily, and at last gave him his victory over her spirit by letting her shoulders wilt in defeat.

Oddly, rather than pleasing him it seemed to have the opposite effect, tightening his mouth and putting an impatient glint into his strange green eyes.

'Look,' he exhaled irritably, 'why don't you avail yourself of some of that coffee? You are obviously jet lagged and no doubt dehydrated. Please...' He waved a hand towards the trolley, but when she still just stood there, looking like a slowly wilting flower, another sigh rasped from him and he came to grasp her arm, guiding her to one of the chairs and pushing her roughly into it.

Annie glanced at the hand on her arm, long-fingered and beautifully sculptured, then at his face, darkly intense and intimidatingly grim, and shivered, realising just how accurate her first impression of this man had been. Danger, her instincts had warned her. Danger—hard with resolve.

Dangerous on several levels, she acknowledged as her senses quivered beneath his touch. Then, as she let her tense body relax into the chair, she was filled with a sudden aching kind of sadness. For the first time in her adult life she had come upon a man whom she did not feel an instant physical revulsion for, and he wanted only to do her harm.

Lifting her hand, she began rubbing at her brow with weary fingers. Her head was beginning to ache, the long hours of travelling only to be faced with all of...this beginning to take their toll.

A minute later a cup of strong coffee was placed into her hand, then he stood over her, with those piercing eyes probing her pale face while she sipped at the strong, sweet drink.

'Please explain the rest,' she requested, once the drink had managed to warm a small part of her numbed body.

He looked ready to refuse, an oddly ferocious look tightening his lean face. Then, on a short sigh, he turned away. 'Hanson will get his exclusive for his magazine,' he assured her. 'Only—' he turned back to face her '—it won't be you wearing the Adamas collection, it will be Susie—after Hanson has begged me to allow her to take your place, of course, when you don't turn up in time for his deadline because you have disappeared with your lover.'

'You, I suppose.' Her smile was twisted with contempt.

'Of course.' He gave an arrogant half-nod of his dark head. 'It has to be convincing, after all. The man may have overstretched his resources in this economic climate, but he is no fool. He knows you well enough to suspect anything less than your assurance that the love of a very rich man has brought this decision on you.'

He paused, waiting for her to put up a protest or at least show some horrified response to his demands. But when she revealed nothing—nothing whatsoever—his frown came back, the first hint of puzzlement showing on his rock-solid, certain face.

'You understand what I am demanding of you?' he questioned. 'I am demanding that you cut yourself completely free of Hanson—both professionally and personally. No contact,' he made clear. 'Nothing. He loves my cousin, but he suffers an incurable lust for you. You cannot be allowed to go on ruining lives simply because that body of yours drives men insane!'

And whose fault is that? she wondered cynically. Mine for projecting exactly what they want to see? Or theirs for being such pathetic slaves to their wretched libidos?

She glanced at him from beneath her lashes, wondering curiously if this man had ever been a slave to his libido. And decided not. He was Adamas—the rock, the invincible one! And just too damned proud to let himself become a slave to anything—except his family, maybe.

And there, she realised suddenly, was his weakness! Hers was Todd and always would be Todd. His was his pride and abiding love for his family.

'You know...' she murmured thoughtfully, a small seed of an idea beginning to develop in her mind. If it worked—if she could swing it—there was a small chance that she could get herself out of this relatively un-scathed. 'You've forgotten one rather obvious thing in all your careful planning,' she said. 'If, by your reck-oning, I've had Todd at my beck and call for the last four years, despite the countless other men he knows have been falling in and out of my bed—then he isn't going to give up on me just because you've come along.'

That deep sense of personal pride took the shape of haughty arrogance on his face. 'He will if I insist upon it,' he said.

'Enough to make him turn to Susie for comfort?' she charged. 'Enough to make him thrust me from his mind? I'm sorry—' ruefully she shook her head '—but it won't happen. Todd loves me, you see,' she stated with a soft and sincere certainty. 'Loves me from the heart not the body. Or why else do you think he keeps coming back to me no matter what goes on in my life?

'Ask Susie if you don't believe me,' she prompted when deriding scepticism that anyone could love a pro-miscuous bitch like her turned his attractive mouth ugly. 'Ask her why all her other attempts to make Todd dismiss me from his life have failed. And ask yourself why a beautiful, desirable woman like Susie cannot win her man on her terms without having to bring you in to do it for her.

'Ask her—' she gently thrust her strongest point home '—if she's ever asked Todd why he refuses to give me up, and if she's honest, Mr DeSanquez, she'll tell you that she *has* asked him, and Todd had told her, quite clearly, that he loves me and will always love me until the day he dies—no matter what I do.'

Silence. She had him wondering, and Annie had to stifle the urge to smile in triumph. The way his sleek black brows were pulling downwards over the bridge of his long, thin nose told her that she had forced him to consider what she'd said.

'You could keep me here for six months—a year! but when I eventually went back Todd would be waiting for me with open arms. Is Susie prepared to live with that?' she challenged. 'Knowing that, no matter how deeply she manages to inveigle Todd into her clutches, I will always be there like the shadowed wings of a hawk in their lives, waiting to swoop down and steal him right away from her?'

This felt good—really good! Annie thought with relish as he spun restlessly away. He poured another drink, swallowed it down in one go then turned, forcing her to smooth the pleased glow out of her eyes as he glanced sharply back at her.

'You really are the shrewd, calculating bitch my family label you, are you not?' he said grimly.

'I am what I am.' She shrugged, throwing his own words of earlier right back at him.

'And what made you what you are, I wonder?' he mused angrily.

'Oh, that's easy,' she said. 'There's a final ingredient in all of this which should clear that up.' She looked him straight in the eye. 'You see, I love Todd in exactly the same way that he loves me. Only, we are not allowed to show it because of Todd's mother. You do know who Todd's mother is, don't you?' she questioned tauntingly.

'She is Lady Sarah Hanson,' she provided the answer whether he knew it or not. 'A woman with pure blue aristocratic blood running through her veins. She would die rather than see her son align himself with a woman with my reputation.' Her soft mouth twisted on that little truism.

'Lady Sarah also suffers from a chronic heart condition,' she went on. Most of this was the absolute truth—most of it. 'Todd is strong—tough—but draws the line at killing his own mother.' She gave a helpless shrug. 'Your Susie doesn't stand a chance against a love like ours, Mr DeSanquez,' she concluded, 'and you would be doing her a bigger service by telling her that, rather than trying to blackmail me.'

At that she got up, mentally crossing her fingers that she'd managed to swing it. He was certainly not as confident as he had been, nor—oddly—as contemptuous of her as he studied her thoughtfully.

'No.' He shook his dark head and her heart sank. 'You are wrong. I have seen the way he looks at my cousin, and no matter what you believe about his feelings for you Hanson gazes at her like a man angrily frustrated in love. Whatever hold you may have on him, and I do not deny it is there,' he conceded, 'I think it is time— perhaps more than time—that both you and Hanson learned to forget each other.

'I saw the way you were with him the other night, watched the seductive way you utterly bewitched him, seducing him with your promising smiles and the sensual brush of your exquisite body.' Contemptuously his gaze raked over her. 'Susie has a chance with him with you out of the way,' he concluded. 'She stands none while you are around.'

'So what is your plan?' she scoffed at him deridingly, her mind tumbling over itself in an effort to find the hidden key that would stop all of this. 'To keep me here tonight and tomorrow night and the next and the next in the hopes that it will blacken me in his eyes? Didn't you hear a word I said?' she sighed. 'Todd doesn't care what I do or who I do it with! He will forgive me for you and he will forgive me for breaking my contract with *Cliché*!'

'Then you have a rather big problem on your hands, Miss Lacey,' he countered grimly. 'Because if you do not find a way of convincing him that you care nothing for him any more then I withdraw my support for his magazine. So now what do you suggest that we do?'

Catch twenty-two. Annie felt her heart sink in her breast.

CHAPTER FIVE

'I SEE I have managed to silence that quick little tongue of yours,' he taunted when the silence stretched out between them. 'But I would appreciate a suggestion as to how we overcome the stalemate we seem to have created.'

'I don't have one,' Annie admitted dully, eyes lowered so that he wouldn't see the frustration glittering there.

'I see,' he said silkily. 'Then it seems to be up to me to find it for you. That is, of course,' he then prompted, 'if you are prepared to do anything to save Hanson from ruin?'

'Yes,' she whispered, with a numbness that encompassed her whole being.

'I beg your pardon?' he drawled aggravatingly, coming to lean over her, bracing his hands on the arms of her chair. 'Was that a yes? I did not quite catch the word.'

'Yes—it was a yes!' she flared, her fingers clenching into tight fists of frustration on her lap. 'I'll do anything to save Todd from ruin!' Then, on a sudden flood of tears that blurred her beautiful eyes, she choked, 'Anything, damn you—anything!'

It was odd, but the tears seemed to throw him. His eyes widened, shocked surprise showing on his lean face before he suddenly jerked away from her as if those tears held poison in them and he was afraid of dying if they so much as touched his skin.

But anyone who knew Annie well would also have known that when tears flowed from her eyes so did her temper burn up to counteract them, and she jumped from her seat, those same tears glistening with a wretched, bitter anger.

'So what do you want me to do?' she demanded shrilly. 'Strip naked in public in the hopes I'll make him despise me? Or simply cut my own throat and put a quick end to all poor Susie's problems? Or maybe,' she went on while he just seemed to stand there struck by her sudden explosion, 'you would like me to strip naked in public *and* cut my own throat? That should do it!' she concluded thickly. 'Put a neat if messy end to the whole bloody lot!'

'Swearing doesn't help,' he said, as if that one expletive was the only part of what she'd thrown at him that had actually meant anything at all.

'Hah!' she choked, her temper almost shooting right out of the top of her head, then disappearing suddenly when she began to see the black humour of the situation. Here she was, offering to top herself for that cat Susie's sake! She couldn't believe that she could be sunk so low!

'I do not think we need take such drastic action—on either point,' he added calmly.

Or was it calmingly? Annie focused her eyes on him at last, wary of the expression on his face that was neither gleeful nor, as she would have expected, contemptuous, but strangely—

No. She spun her back on him, arms wrapping tightly around her body in an age-old gesture of self-defence. She refused so much as to put a word to what her senses had told her that new look in his eyes meant!

'Then what the hell *do* you want me to do?' she muttered thickly.

There was a silence behind her that made the fine nerves lying along her spine prickle. She closed her eyes tightly, refusing—refusing to listen to what her senses were screaming at her. It was impossible. No man could find it arousing to have a woman swap insults with him! No woman could find it arousing to spar with a man like him!

Yet—

Oh, God, if he touched her now... And she could feel him fighting the urge to do just that, feel it with every instinct she possessed buzzing in warning that he was—

'You must convince Hanson that I mean more to you than he does.' The words came from a throat roughened by the battle he had just fought with himself and won. 'You must make him believe that I am the man who has managed to take his place in your heart!'

Annie had to swallow to clear the tension from her throat. 'And how am I supposed to do that?' she asked, without turning to face him. She didn't dare.

Didn't dare.

Another loaded pause shifted the tension upwards another notch. Then he said quietly, 'In two weeks Hanson will arrive here at my invitation. You will first convince him that you and I have become—passionate lovers, then I will hand him an envelope which will supposedly contain the photographs he desires so much. But before he has a chance to open it you will take it from him and rip it in two.'

'*What*?' That made her turn, her blue eyes dark with confusion as she levelled them at him. 'But what is that going to prove?' she gasped.

'It will prove that your love for me means more to you than your love for him, because you are prepared to ruin him rather than lose me. You see,' he went on, turning slightly to pick up his glass, 'I will have issued you with a decision to make. You can save him and lose me, or ruin him and have me. You will, of course, choose me.'

'But—I thought the whole point of all of this was *not* to ruin Todd?' she choked, utterly bewildered now.

'No—no,' he denied. 'The whole point of all of this is to pay you back for the ruin you have wrought in others' lives and to get you out of Hanson's life,' he corrected. 'And your taking away his best chance at success at the eleventh hour should alienate you completely,' he decreed with grim satisfaction.

'But will also lose you my agreement to co-operate,' she said. 'Or have you forgotten that I'm only doing this for Todd's sake?'

'No.' He shook his dark head. 'I have not forgotten. But you seem to have forgotten my cousin Susie waiting in the wings to step neatly into your shoes. Co-operate, and she will convince me to let her take your place. Susie will wear the Adamas collection for *Cliché*'s European launch, save Hanson from ruin and receive his undying gratitude in the interim. Refuse to co-operate,' he added smoothly, 'and I will simply keep you here out of harm's way until the very last moment—then pull out of the deal—' he gave an idle shrug '—leaving him with nothing—nothing to fall back on. You understand?'

Understand? Oh, yes, she understood, Annie thought bitterly. Susie gets everything at Annie Lacey's expense.

'My God!' she breathed. 'You're worse than Svengali, aren't you? And what happens to me once this little charade is all over?' she asked. 'Am I supposed to keep my mouth shut about the way you and Susie plotted this whole thing against me? Because I won't, Mr DeSanquez,' she warned him angrily. 'And by then *Cliché* will be launched and you won't be able to hurt Todd!'

His answering sigh was harsh and driven. 'Why can you not possess enough simple decency to see without the threats that it is time you let go of Hanson—for his sake if not your own?'

'You talk to me about decency,' she countered scathingly. 'Where is yours while you stand here threatening me like this?'

'You need teaching a lesson,' he muttered, but she knew that her words had got through to him because he dropped his gaze from hers.

'Not in Susie Frazer's name, I don't,' she denied. 'And you're wrong to do this to me and wrong to do this to Todd simply on the evidence of that silly, deranged woman!'

Wrong thing to say, Annie realised as anger flared into his vivid green eyes and he took a threatening step towards her. 'You will take that back!' he insisted, thrusting his dark face close to her own.

For once he looked and sounded completely foreign—hard and dark and frighteningly alien, his anger so palpable that she could almost taste it. Annie quailed inside but refused to show it, her blue eyes clinging defiantly to his.

'I will take nothing back!' she spat at him. 'In your arrogant self-righteousness you like to believe that I've sinned against your rotten family when in reality it is they who've sinned against me!'

'Sin?' he repeated. 'You are sin, Annie Lacey. With your siren's body and your lush, lying mouth.'

'The lies are all yours, Adamas,' she threw back. 'And what do you think it will do to Susie's chances when Todd finds out what a lie this whole thing actually is?'

'And you intend to tell him so?' he demanded.

Annie stood firm in her defiance. 'What do you expect me to do once this is all over?' she snapped. 'Crawl into some dark corner and pretend I no longer exist? I have a life waiting for me out there, Mr DeSanquez. You can put it on hold for a few short weeks but not for ever! And, my God, I vow that the first thing I'll do with that life is save Todd from Susie's calculating clutches if it becomes the very last thing I am able to do!'

His anger shot up another notch, sent there, she suspected, by sheer frustration with her for defying him like this. 'By telling Hanson the truth?' He was demanding confirmation.

'About your lies? Yes!' she declared.

His hand whipped out, curling threateningly around the back of her neck. 'Then we will have to make the lies the truth,' he gritted, moving close so that his body pressed along the full length of hers. His breath was warm against her face, his green eyes glowing with a new and terrifyingly readable light. 'I shall bed you if I have to, Angelica Lacey,' he told her huskily. 'I will take your beautiful body and drown in its sinful lusts every night for the next two weeks if you continue to insist on telling the truth.'

'No,' she protested, trying to move away from him. The heat from his body was having a strange effect on her own, burning it, bringing it to life, disturbing all those delicate senses she had always so thoroughly locked away.

'Why not?' he whispered. 'Why not make the charade the truth? Two weeks is a long time for a woman like you to go without a man. And I find I am man enough to be—receptive to your charms. Why not?' he repeated, almost as though he was trying to convince himself rather than her. His mouth lowered to brush a tantalising caress along her cheek. 'I can feel you trembling,' he murmured. 'I can feel your breasts throbbing against my chest, smell the sweet scent of desire on your skin. You want me, Angelica.'

'No—'

'Yes,' he insisted. 'As much as I admit to wanting you.'

'No—' she denied again, trying to pull free because he was conjuring up all kinds of sensations that were totally, frighteningly foreign to her.

'You want proof?' Reaching down, he took hold of her tightly clenched hands and grimly prised the fingers apart before forcing by sheer superior strength her tense palm to press against the hardening muscle between his thighs. 'Proof,' he muttered, and captured her shaken gasp with his hungry mouth.

For a few blinding, ecstatic moments Annie let herself sink willingly into the embrace, some small, sensible corner of her brain telling her that this had been coming from the moment they'd met the night before, that the violent exchange of words had merely been a vent for... this—this sudden greedy need to feel his mouth on hers again, to feel his body pulse against her, know his touch, his taste, the texture of his tight, tanned skin.

But it was only for a few hectic moments, then an icy darkness began closing her in—the darkness of bad memories, of man's physical power over woman and his ability to subdue her if she dared to protest.

And suddenly, instead of the warm, coaxing mouth of the man kissing her now, she was being stifled by the hot, wet pressure of another mouth—a cruel mouth—and cruel hands that hurt as they touched her. Hands which had her crying out, fighting for breath, straining to get free, struggling—struggling so desperately that she didn't even know that she was flailing wildly at César DeSanquez with her fists, didn't realise that he was no longer kissing her but frowning down at her, no longer holding her in an embrace but trying—unsuccessfully—to stop her from landing blows on his surprised face.

'Angel—'

It was all she heard. Not the full 'Angelica' he had actually said in husky concern but 'Angel' as Luis had husked at her—'Angel. I have a real angel in my bed.'

'No!' she ground out, and managed at last to break free, her blue eyes wild as she turned like a terrified animal and ran.

Ran out of the open windows across the veranda and down the wooden steps. Ran—ran with no idea where she was running as her feet took her across the springy grass still warm from the long day's sun. It was almost dark outside now, but she didn't notice—didn't notice anything as she made her mindless bid for escape.

She came to a halt only when the balmy water of the Caribbean lapped around her thighs. Breathless from running, panting with fear, she lifted her dazed eyes to the miles of coral-washed water laid out in front of her and at last felt reality return.

Not Luis Alvarez but César DeSanquez. Not the darkened bedroom of a plush London penthouse but a Caribbean island basking in the embrace of a beautiful dying sun.

'Oh, God,' she choked out thickly. 'Oh, God.' And, limp-limbed suddenly, she dropped like a weighted sack onto her knees, then as the water closed in a lazy, silken swirl around her heaving shoulders she put her hands to her face and wept.

Whatever he would do about her stupid flight she didn't consider, but certainly she didn't expect him to come wading into the water after her, his dark eyes tight with fury as he hauled her angrily to her feet and began dragging her back onto dry land again.

It was only later that it occurred to her that it might well have looked to him as if she were trying to drown herself. Whatever, it gained her no sympathy whatsoever—no hint of remorse as he muttered something harsh and Spanish beneath his breath then picked her up in his arms and carried her back up the garden towards the house.

His step hardly altered as he carried her up a flight of steps that led up the outside wall of the house and along the upper balcony into a room where he dropped her onto her unsteady feet before stalking off towards what she vaguely assumed was a bathroom.

Because this was a bedroom, she realised on yet another rise of panic—a bedroom with two full-length windows standing open either side of a huge coral-pink covered bed.

'Get those wet things off!' He came back with a fluffy white towel. Annie started, her blue eyes huge in her pale face as she stared blankly at him, unable to move a single muscle in case she fell down again.

With another Spanish curse he began stripping off her clothes, the bite of his fingers quelling any attempt she made at trying to stop him. She was shivering violently, though with shock rather than cold. Her top came off and was thrown down on the soft coral-coloured carpet, her arms wrenched away when they automatically crossed over her breasts. With rough hands he unclipped her bra and sent that flying too.

Then, as she stood there still half-numbed by her mind-blowing reaction to his kiss, the towel landed around her shoulders and he was kneeling in front of her, dark face stern as he ruthlessly began to strip the dripping wet skirt from her, followed instantly by her briefs.

'You stupid fool,' he bit out hoarsely. 'What made you do something as crazy as that?'

She didn't answer—couldn't. She just stood there huddling into the towel and shivering so badly that her teeth chattered. He cursed again, turning angrily away, and began wrenching off his own sodden clothes. His trousers landed on top of her skirt, the sleek, lean flanks of his buttocks flexing as he stripped away his briefs and sent them the same way before spinning back to face her, arrogant in his complete lack of modesty and misreading her new, white-faced stillness as indifference to his exposure while he railed at her once again.

'I should throttle the lovely life out of you for doing something as stupid as that!'

With another rasping sigh he turned and walked back into the bathroom while Annie stood staring after him, mesmerised by those exposed buttocks rippling as he moved. He came back with another towel, his face no less angry as he stripped his shirt over his head and slammed it down onto the floor.

And Annie lost the ability to breathe.

Her eyes were fixed unblinkingly on that daunting juncture between muscle-taut thighs where the shadowing of crisp black chest hair arrowed to a thick cluster around his potent sex.

He obviously felt no qualms about standing stark naked in front of Annie Lacey. As far as he was concerned, she had seen it all before—many times. But to her this was one of the most critical occasions of her life. And she could neither move, breathe nor speak as, dry-mouthed, she stared at him, horrified by the slow, rumbling burn beginning to erupt deep down inside her.

Desire—for a man who held her in such contempt. And a fascination so strong that she couldn't even make herself look the other way! Her eyes flickered, then shifted to graze over wide shoulders and bulging biceps where the deeply tanned skin shone like lovingly oiled leather.

His chest was wide and firm, covered by the thick mass of black curling hair—hair that angled down over a stomach so tight that she felt she could throw a punch at it and not make it give so much as a fraction. Then those hips—those narrow, tight hips so arrogantly cradling the essence of the man himself, a man endowed with such power that she could almost feel its—

'*Santa María . . .*'

The softly uttered words barely impinged on her concentration. She was too lost in what was happening to him, too busy watching in paralysed awe as his body stirred, hardened, grew into full masculine arousal.

He let go of the towel and began walking slowly towards her. Annie took in a short, shaky breath and moistened her dry lips with her tongue. She couldn't move, was unable to do anything other than watch him fill with desire, and feel her own senses fill with the same.

'Sin,' he muttered tightly as his eyes glittered over her. 'You are sin, Angelica Lacey. Pure sin.'

Coming to a stop in front of her, his hand lifted, stroking across her shoulder on its way to capture the edge of her towel. She was trembling when it fell away—not shivering now, but most definitely trembling. There was a subtle difference, and it all had to do with the sensations she was experiencing inside.

His hand was on her waist, gripping, tugging—arrogant in his maleness as he lifted her up against him. She arched on an indrawn gasp as his manhood slid proudly between her trembling thighs. For a moment they stayed like that, their eyes locked, burning, darkened by feeling. Then he captured her parted mouth, widened it and plunged hungrily in.

And she surrendered—surrendered to the storm that had been building steadily from the moment their eyes had clashed across a crowded room...

Nothing—nothing in her vast and cynical if second-hand knowledge about the act of love had prepared her for what had actually taken place there in the growing darkness of that night.

Nothing. And she lay very still beside the man who had just propelled her into true womanhood, not daring to move while she came to terms with the wreck it had left of her emotions—her senses! Her very soul.

César was lying beside her, stretched out on his stomach, his arms curved tensely around his dark head. His body was damp, layered with a fine film of perspiration. His shoulders, his hips, his slim, tight buttocks were trembling as he struggled to come to terms with what had just taken place.

He was shocked.

Dear God, *she* was shocked! But both for different reasons. She was shocked by the sheer, brutal reality of the act. His shock came from discovering that the woman he had just taken with such devastating power and sensuality was not the woman he had believed her to be.

And why should he have suspected? she asked herself bitterly. She was the notorious Annie Lacey, for goodness' sake. Used—more than used to experiencing what they had just done!

She had not even attempted to tell him the truth.

And would he have believed the truth if she had attempted to tell him?

Of course not. Who would? She was Annie Lacey. A product of her own making. She had set out to build a lie around herself and had succeeded so successfully that no one ever thought of questioning that lie.

But he could have been—kinder, she thought on a sudden well of anguish. No matter who or what he'd believed her to be, he still could have been kinder— couldn't he?

Tears lay like a film across her eyes, blurring her vision as the moon filtered through the darkness of the room. She hurt. She hurt in so many places that she did not know which one hurt the most—her body, still wearing the power of his physical imprint, her brain, grinding against her skull in stunned revelation, her senses, still quivering, flailing around in the morass of the aftermath, not quite knowing what had happened to them, and too shattered by it all even to attempt to regroup.

Then a hand reached out to touch her, and everything—mind, body, shattered senses—leapt upwards and together in a wild dovetailing of panic, sending her rolling from the bed to land, swaying, on her feet—feet that were already stumbling away, running from what she knew was bound to come next.

The post-mortem. No! Please! Just let me be!

Bathroom. A bathroom door had a lock on it, and she needed to put herself behind lock and key before he—

'Angelica . . .'

No! Bright balls of panic propelled themselves against the back of her eyes, and in one swift movement she leapt like a gazelle into the bathroom, closing and locking the door behind her before sliding heavily down its smooth, panelled white surface onto the cold, hard ceramic-tiled floor.

Her knees came up, her arms wrapping tensely around them, then her head was lowering, the silken tangle of her hair falling like a curtain all around her as she sat huddled, shivering. Exposed.

Exposed for exactly what she was.

A fraud.

For the last four years of her life she had been a complete fraud. She, the shrewd and cynical Annie Lacey, who had believed that she was playing a great game with other people's perception of her, now realised that she had only been deceiving herself. In her way, she'd believed that she was punishing them all for making her be that way when in actual fact she had been punishing herself—punishing herself for a whole range of things, Alvarez being only a small part in all of that, she now realised.

He had been the conductor, but not the whole orchestra.

'Oh, God.' The words came choking from a throat closed tight on tears of self-knowledge.

You hate yourself, Annie, she told herself wretchedly—not all those other people who only responded to what you gave them to respond to. You built Annie Lacey because you truly believe that persona the only one you're fit for.

Woman as whore. She shuddered nauseously. The fact that you never actually did whore around is incidental. It is what you believed yourself to be.

And now you are, she added starkly—the whore of a man who despises everything about you, even the fact that he could not stop himself from devouring the body he despised so much.

'Sin'. He had called her 'sin'.

'Angelica.' A tap at the door behind her accompanied the gruff reverberation of her name. 'Angelica, open the door.'

No. God, no, she thought, and stumbled to her feet, blue eyes so dark with emotion that they seemed black in her paste-white face. Sheer instinct sent her towards the glass door which housed the shower cubicle. She stepped in and switched on the jet, not caring that the water hissed down icy cold on top of her, then almost immediately stinging-hot.

The need to wash away the whole experience kept her locked beneath the shower, lost to everything but a grinding knowledge of utter self-disgust.

If he knocked or called her name again, she didn't hear him. And she stayed like that for long, long minutes, face lowered, water streaming onto her head until her long hair split and hung in two slick golden pelts from her nape.

Then, slowly, a sense of feeling began to creep back into her numbed flesh, the hot sting of water pulsing down on her urging her back to life, and she lifted her head, found a bar of soap and began methodically washing herself. Toes, feet, legs. Her thighs where his thrusting body had left marks on her fine, delicate skin.

She washed her hips and her buttocks—sore where the height of his passion had sent his fingers digging in. The smell of him and the feel of him still lingered languorously in the hot, steamy air.

Her belly felt tight and tender inside, her breasts alien parts of her that, when she smoothed soap over the taut, swollen mounds, brought a sharp gasp of reaction from her tight throat as her fingers brushed nipples still erect and raw from his hot, hungry kisses.

He had left his mark here in other ways too—in reddened blotches where his lips had nipped and sucked. Her throat had the same—several tender places where she knew she would bruise later on. It was the way of her skin—pale, delicate, it bruised at the slightest knock.

Her arms seemed to be the only part of her that had escaped the marks of his possession—except for her wrists, she noted as she stared at them, ringed pink where he had gripped them together over her head. Oh, not in a demand for submission, she grimly allowed, but in rough, angry passion. He'd wanted to stretch her out to her fullest so that he could taste every inch of her skin with his tongue, kneeling over her with his dark face fierce with desire.

A ripple fluttered over her skin—in memory of the pleasure he had given. Her mouth, full and throbbing, was still wearing his kisses even though she had washed her lips as well.

Sighing, she turned her face up to the spray then stood there with her eyes closed, trying not to think of it any more.

Then her nails curled tensely into her palms as unwillingly she remembered what she had done to him, how the wild explosion of passion inside her had sent her fingers raking across his sleekly groomed head, searching for, finding and clutching at the slim tail of hair, then tugging—using it to pull him closer so that she could lose herself in his hot, marauding mouth.

Then later... She shuddered, remembering how those same fingers had scraped the ribbon right away, his hair falling like midnight silk around her as her fingers had moved on again, curling into tense claws to score down the full length of his long, muscular back as he'd entered her... Her impassioned cry of pain echoed now in the hollow place her mind had become.

Well, there was one thing, she mocked herself grimly when eventually she made herself move again, she had gone from virgin to experienced lover in one fell swoop, because there had been nothing that he hadn't shown her in that wildly hectic romp on the bed, nothing he had not been prepared to do to heighten their pleasure.

No gentle introduction for the virgin. No holds barred.

That point between her thighs quivered in response, and jerkily she pushed herself out of the shower before it all took too frightening a grip on her again.

Another huge white bath sheet hung folded on the rail. Picking it up, she wrapped it fully around herself then found another towel which she wrapped turban-style round her head.

It took a teeth-clenching gathering together of all her courage to make her unlock the door and step back into the bedroom.

CHAPTER SIX

CÉSAR WAS still there, standing by the open window on the other side of the bed, gazing out at a moonlit sea. He was dressed again, in a fresh white shirt and a pair of casual trousers. His hair had been severely contained once again.

Like the man, she decided hollowly—back under control.

Someone had removed the wet clothes, and the bed had been tidied. Not that it mattered. Nothing mattered.

Ignoring him, she moved over to a big, apricot-coloured easy chair and, snatching up the scatter cushion lying on it, sat down, curling herself into it, hugging the cushion to her breasts.

'Why?' he demanded quietly—nothing else. It really was not necessary to add anything else.

'People see what they want to see,' she answered flatly. She could have said more but didn't. She didn't want to talk at all. She just wanted to sit here and wallow in the aftermath of a holocaust.

He moved, turning his tense body a little so that he could look at her. The movement made her glance warily at him, her huge blue eyes that had lost all their self-protecting veils clashing with a tight, grim face emptied of most of its beautiful colour. He was holding his lips in a straight, tight line, as if the teeth behind them were fiercely clenched, his chiselled jaw set under the pressure.

His eyes were dark and sombre, the truth overlaying his earlier contempt with remorse.

No. She looked down and away again as compassion for him began to swell inside her. But she was too full with her own dark thoughts just now to deal with his.

And anyway, even though she was aware that maybe half of the blame for what had taken place between them had to lie at her own feet—or those of the Annie Lacey she had so carefully deceived everyone with—she could not forgive him his soulless seduction.

Would not forgive him.

He had got her here to this island under false pretences. He had insulted and threatened her, then coolly blackmailed her before offering the final indignity of ruthlessly seducing her.

If he'd wanted his revenge, he had it. She only hoped that he was satisfied with his results.

Oh, God help me, she thought on a sudden well of absolute despair, and began to sob softly, brokenly into the protection of the cushion.

'Hell.' The thickened curse came from very close by. He was squatting down in front of her. 'I'm sorry,' he murmured deeply. 'What else can I say? I swear to you, I never meant to hurt you like this.'

No? He had set out to hurt her from the very moment they'd met. If it hadn't been this way then it would have been another. He'd seen only the persona, which made the rest of what had happened such a sick joke because, in the end, even he hadn't been able to keep his hands off Annie Lacey, the super-tramp.

And the angry way he'd lost control of himself had told her just how much he'd despised himself for it.

'Leave me alone,' she whispered. 'I just w-want to be left alone.'

He sighed, the heavy sound disturbing the air around her naked shoulders and she shivered.

'You're cold,' he said, with a kind of rough gentleness that made her want to weep all the more. 'Let me help you into bed, then I will—'

'No!' His hand had come out to touch her; she reared away from him like a terrified animal. Her tear-washed face came out of the cushion, and in sheer self-preservation Annie Lacey surged furiously back to life. 'You've had what you wanted from me—now get out of here. *Get out*!'

Eyes as dark as the ocean beyond the window held onto stormy blue. He didn't flinch from the contempt she seared at him, did not respond to it. And for a moment out of time they stayed like that, he squatting there while she leaned accusingly towards him.

The damner being damned.

But even as she huddled there, flaying him with her eyes, she felt the lazy beginnings of other emotions start to flutter into corrupting life. Her pulse began to race, her aching breasts to stir, her senses pumping soft, sensual messages to the muscles around her sex.

His fault! He had done this to her—awoken demons she had believed so thoroughly shut away! And she hated him for that too, because it showed that no matter how degrading the revelation that had taken place in this room, she'd liked it, and wanted more.

Oh, God. 'Get out of here, you bastard,' she whispered thickly, and lowered her face again—though her senses were on full alert. Bastard he might be, but a proud one. And she was sure that he would not take kindly to having the word spat into his face.

Yet—he did take it; with only another heavy sigh he took it and drew himself grimly to his feet. 'At least get yourself into bed, Angelica,' he advised quietly. 'Or you will catch a chill sitting there like that. I will send Margarita up with some food.' He was walking towards the door. 'Perhaps by tomorrow you will be ready to talk. I will see you then.'

Annie waited until she heard the quiet click as the door closed behind him before she began crying all over again.

She was sitting on a rock, gazing emptily out to sea, when the skittering displacement of a pebble somewhere behind her warned her that she was no longer alone.

It was still quite early. Having surprisingly slept the sleep of the dead the night before, she had awoken just as dawn had been turning the sky from navy to blue. And on a restless urge to stop the events of the previous night from tumbling back into her head she'd got up, dressed in a simple pair of white shorts and a white T-shirt, then left her room via the French windows.

Glancing up, she saw César coming towards her. Barefoot, he moved easily across the light, pebbly ground, the solid gold bracelet of his watch glinting in the early morning light. Behind him his white-painted house stood in the shadow of a new day. Behind it stood the hill, with its thicket of trees reaching up towards a pure blue sky.

A beautiful place. Somewhere between Eden and paradise, she found herself thinking fancifully.

If César was the serpent Annie wasn't sure what that made her.

He was dressed in a light cambric shirt and a pair of thin white cotton beach trousers rolled up a little at the ankles. His hair was contained, his face wearing the sheen of a man who had just indulged in a close shave, and he looked devastatingly attractive.

A man who stood out on his own as special.

No. Firmly she squashed what was trying to take place inside her, and looked away again. She did not want to feel anything right now.

And she did not want to see the knowledge that she knew would be written in his shrewd emerald eyes if she let her own eyes clash with them.

He came to drop down beside her. No smile, no greeting—no tension in him. He simply drew up his knees, spread them slightly, rested his deeply tanned forearms on top, and said, 'Right. It is time for explanations, Angelica. I want to know what made you into the absolute fraud you are.'

Just like that. She smiled to herself. Guilt and remorse done with the night before, he now demanded enlightenment.

'Looking for absolution, Mr DeSanquez?' she asked. 'You won't get it, you know,' she warned him. 'All you will do is discover that you are just like the rest of the human race—rarely looking beyond what you're expecting to see.'

'And you with your carefully prepared persona did not aid that deception?' he countered.

Annie's shoulders moved in a careless shrug. 'I am in the business of selling things,' she reminded him.

'Using your notoriety to do it.'

'A commodity you weren't above exploiting yourself to help sell your precious collection. Which,' she added before he could say anything else, 'I accept entirely as part of my job. But it never occurred to you to look beyond the façade to the real person beneath.'

'It wasn't merely the false image which made you the woman I saw you to be, Angelica,' he argued. 'There were other, far more convincing factors which did that. Alvarez, for instance,' he prompted quietly.

'Alvarez', she noted. Luis Alvarez had suddenly become the detached 'Alvarez' instead of the more familiar 'brother-in-law'.

She almost smiled at the irony of it, only her stiff lips would not stretch to it. Instead she reached down to gather up a handful of pebbles from the side of her rock, then told him grimly, 'I am not going to bare my soul to you just because you've happened to discover my darkest secret.'

'It was not a dark secret, Angelica,' he countered gently. 'It was a sad one.'

Sad. A moment's moisture spread across her eyes then left again.

It was more than sad. It was pathetic, she thought bitterly as her mind flew back to that dark period in her life.

At sixteen years old she had to have been the most naïve female alive. A child actress with a fresh-faced, angelic image that had made people sigh when they'd seen her on their TV sets playing a role that had grown from a single ad for breakfast cereal into a three-year-long concept of how every parent would want their teenage daughter to look and behave.

The first ad had begun simply, with her sitting in a homely kitchen with the morning sunlight beaming down onto her pale gold head. She had been dressed for school in a neat lemon and white striped uniform and her face had shown the horrors that the voice-over had explained she was experiencing with the onset of her first day at a brand new school.

'Eat up,' her TV mother had commanded gently. 'Things won't look half so bad on a full stomach.'

Reluctantly she'd pulled the bowl of crunchy flakes towards her, dipped in her spoon and forced the first mouthful down; the next had not been quite so slow, the one after that almost eager. By the time she had finished the whole bowl her face had firmed, her small chin lifting determinedly, her thoughts—via the voice-over—having become more positive with each mouthful.

The next episode had shown her coming home again, buoyant, alive, rushing into the kitchen to tell her mother about her first exciting day, and all the time she'd chatted the bowl had been coming off the shelf, the crunchy-flake box out of the cupboard, milk from the fridge. Then had come the blissful silence as she'd eaten, blue eyes shining, the voice-over explaining her instant success at her new school as she'd replayed it to her bowl of cereal.

Over the next three years her crunchy cereal, via the voice-over discussions she'd had with it, had solved all her teenage problems with a lesson well learned at the end of each ad, which had earned her the nickname 'The Angel'.

The ads had been thrown up at other teenagers as perfect examples of good moral behaviour. She had been kind to animals, old people and small children. Parents had loved her, grandparents had loved her, small children had loved her—teenagers had hated her. Which was why she'd had so few friends of her own age—that and the fact that she'd lived with an aunt who had kept her strictly to heel when she had not been working or at school.

Losing Aunt Claire at the vulnerable age of nineteen had been like losing the linchpin that had held her un-natural life together. It had also preceded her spec-tacular fall from grace—a fall which had left her with two options only. Either she crawled away to hide in shame or she lifted her chin and outfaced everything that her critics had to throw at her. She had chosen the latter. And, with Todd's support, countless surprise offers had flooded in to Lissa, her agent, for the kind of work which must have made her aunt turn in her grave.

It was only as César's hand reached out to cover her own that she realised she was sitting there pressing damp pebbles between two tense palms as if she were trying to grind them into dust.

She looked down at that hand—big and dark, and seeming to promise so many things that she had learned not to trust. A hand that now knew her more intimately than any hand. The hand that had drawn from her a woman she hadn't known existed inside her.

The hand of contempt, now the hand of consolation.

She pushed it away.

There was a moment's silence, in which they both stared bleakly out to sea. Then, on a soft sigh that revealed an until now banked-down frustration, he requested brusquely, 'At least tell me what Hanson is to you.'

'Todd?' She turned a glance on him, seeing for the first time how his shattered illusions had scored deep grooves of strain into his lean, dark face. He was not so calm and composed, nor was he finished with guilt and remorse, she added as his eyes caught hers and held, the sombre glow of regret dulling the usual incisive greenness. 'Well, he's not my lover, that's for sure,' she drawled with mocking irreverence, watched him wince, then turned her face away again to stare back out to sea.

'He's my half-brother,' she announced.

Well aware that she had just delivered the biggest shock she could have done she selected one of the tiny pebbles in her hand and threw it into the ocean.

'We share the same father,' she extended, launching another pebble. 'Though I didn't find out about him until my aunt died.' She paused, then added, tight-lipped and flatly, 'Only she wasn't my aunt. She was my mother.'

Another stone was launched into the clear blue water while she gave those few pertinent facts a chance to settle in the stunned air surrounding them. Then she quietly began relating a story that she had never told anyone in her life before—though why she suddenly chose to tell this man was beyond her ability to understand.

'Not once during the eighteen years I lived with her did she ever let me know that interesting little fact,' she told him. 'I had to wait until she was dead to discover our true relationship—via letters sent from Todd's father to her, laying out ground rules for the lump sum he settled on us both which involved her holding her silence about his name. Why she decided to include herself in that silence I don't know.' And will never know now, she added bleakly to herself. 'But discovering that far from being the orphan I'd always believed myself to be I'd had not only a mother but a father as well sent me a little crazy for a time.'

'You were hurt,' he defended her gently.

'And the rest,' she said, and huffed out a sound of scorn. Hurt, angry, bitter, betrayed.

She hunched her body over her knees, a fresh handful of pebbles clenched in her fist.

'I stormed into Giles Hanson's office and began shrieking at him like a maniac,' she went on after a moment. 'I accused him of just about everything I could accuse him of, then set about telling him what I thought of him as a man.'

The word 'man' emerged with enough contempt to make any man wince. César winced.

'I had just got to the part where I was telling him how I was going to reveal to the world how he and my mother had treated me when Todd came into the room.'

She turned to look at him then, her gaze skimming over his set, sober face. 'Your eyes are the same colour as Susie's,' she remarked—quite out of context. 'I should have made that connection a lot earlier than I did. And I'm surprised now that I didn't.'

He glanced at her frowningly, not really under-standing what she was getting at. 'We have nothing else in common,' he said, almost as if he was defending himself against a suspected insult. 'The eyes are the only legacy.'

'You think so?' Her expression was curious and damning at the same time. But she didn't elaborate, returning to the original subject instead. 'I took one look at Todd and saw myself,' she said. 'The hair, the eyes... We are so similar, in fact, that I am amazed that no one else has ever made the connection.

'Still—' she shrugged '—I didn't give a hoot about what he looked like then as I slammed into him as well as his father. He was shocked.' She grimaced, remembering that look of pained horror on Todd's face as clearly as if he were standing in front of her right now. 'Shocked enough for me to realise through my rage that he, like myself, knew nothing about his father's past indiscretion.

'But it was he who calmed me down, he who shut his father up when he began spitting all kinds of threats back at me about what would happen if I did open my mouth. And it was Todd who led me out of there, took me to his apartment, let me pour out the whole dirty story all over again, then set about convincing me that I would do no one any good by making it all public, but could actually do a lot of harm.'

Her mouth tightened, eyes glinting at some bitter memory of then that could still hurt her now. 'His mother really does suffer from a chronic heart problem,' she said huskily. 'And finding out about me would surely have killed her because she so foolishly believed that she had a marriage made in heaven.' Her cynicism was so tight and bitter that even Annie wanted to wince when she heard it in her tone.

'Todd didn't care what the scandal could do to his father. But he did care about his mother. So did I, funnily enough,' she admitted. 'Having known what it felt like to be betrayed by just about everyone who should love you, I had no wish to put a sick woman through the same kind of hell. So—' another of those expressive shrugs '—I found myself shut out in the cold again.'

'Hanson shut you out also?' César said in surprise.

'I shut him out actually,' she amended. 'He had his loyalties, which did not include me or my feelings, so as far as I was concerned right then he could go to hell with the rest of them. I told you I'd gone a little crazy,' she reminded him. 'Anger, hurt, bitterness—you name it—' she grimaced '—he got the lot since his father had delegated responsibility to his son.'

'You say "his" father,' César remarked. 'But he was your father also.'

'Not so you'd notice,' she said. 'Not so you'd ever notice,' she then added tightly. 'He died last year never having so much as mentioned my name. Ironic really,' she tagged on ruefully, 'that he should precede his ailing wife to the grave after all he had been prepared to do to me to protect a slowly dying woman from more pain.

'Still—' another shrug '—perhaps that was the price he had to pay for being such a callous, devious swine. I don't regret his going, and I can't say I have any regrets now that he never acknowledged me for what I was to him. He was just a man—' again that contempt for men in general slithered into her tone '—like all the rest of them—vulnerable to his sexual urges but unwilling to accept the consequences of his weakness.'

'So you paid him back for his rejection of you by becoming someone he could never acknowledge even if he did change his mind.'

'The notorious Annie Lacey, you mean?' A soft laugh that fell nowhere near humour left her dry lips. 'Oh, no,' she denied. 'That honour goes to someone much closer to your home, Mr DeSanquez.' She turned her cheek on her arms to look directly at him. 'Luis Alvarez did that.'

He flinched but did not protest, and for a moment she studied the tight line of his profile, wondering how far ahead of her his mind had already taken him. It had to have skipped some way ahead on the simple knowledge that last night had given him. But how far he was willing to use his intelligence to work out the rest, she didn't know.

He was proud—too proud for his own good, probably. That pride might not be willing to take the full brunt of all of this without him at least putting up a token objection—like that of sacrificing her feelings for that of his family.

She knew all about that kind of thing, had experienced it before. She turned away, deciding that it was up to him to indicate whether or not she continued this. The trouble was, she accepted as she launched another stone into the clear blue sea, that what she said was going to make him appear as gullible as a babe in arms, and she had a feeling he knew that too.

'Please continue.'

He was going to take it all on board. Annie smiled grimly to herself.

'I was nineteen years old,' she reminded him, with the first hint of a wobble in her voice. 'And until my aunt— stroke mother,' she added deridingly, 'died I had been kept pretty much to heel by her overprotection and the kind of job I did alongside normal schoolwork.'

Her hands wrapped themselves around her legs again, shoulders hunching in as if to protect her from some unseen evil. 'And, as I told you, discovering all that dirt about myself sent me a little crazy for a time—discos, parties, anything to keep the bitterness away. Then I went to your party. It was *your* party, wasn't it?' She partly asked him, partly accused him.

He sighed heavily in answer, a nerve clenching at the side of his jaw. 'I was in London on business,' he explained. 'I happened to see you on television—playing a cameo role in a big period drama...'

Annie nodded, knowing exactly what drama he was referring to. It had been the first real acting role she'd been offered—and it had turned out to be the last, because her life had blown apart not long after that drama had been shown on TV.

'You were so beautiful,' he murmured gruffly, 'that I wanted to meet you. I knew the director. He promised to bring you to a party I was giving at my apartment.'

'You weren't there,' Annie stated with an absolute certainty. She would have known, she was sure of it. She would know if this man was in the same hemisphere as herself.

'I was called away on urgent business,' he said, confirming his absence. 'My sister and her husband were staying with me at the apartment. They offered to play host to my guests in my place, but Cristina was taken ill early on and apparently took to her bed, leaving Luis to play host alone.'

'Which is why I met him there instead of you.' She swallowed thickly, and lowered her face to watch her hand grind tiny pebbles in her palm again.

'You were starving for affection.' He turned his head to look at her with dark and sombre eyes. 'He offered it. You grabbed at it desperately with both hands.'

About to throw her fistful of stones, Annie paused to stare at him. 'You are joking, of course,' she gasped. 'He was old enough to be my father!'

César nodded. 'The father-figure you had been deprived of all your life.'

That made her laugh, not humorously but with a wincing mockery. 'He was a dissolute slob,' she derided with contempt, 'who tricked me into that bedroom then proceeded to attack me!'

She was on her feet suddenly, wiping her damp palms down her thighs in a tense, agitated kind of way that said she was reliving that dreadful moment in her life.

'He would have succeeded in raping me too,' she added thickly, 'if his wife hadn't walked in the room!'

And suddenly she was shaking, white-faced, the whole length of her slender frame from the top of her head to her curled toes trembling with a painful mixture of anger and sickening repugnance.

'But if this is true—why did you not tell someone?' He made a sharp, uncontrolled gesture of pained disgust that brought him jerkily to his feet. 'Call in the police?'

For that Annie turned a withering look of contempt on him. 'Are you really that naïve about your family?' she cried. 'Your sister was there, for goodness' sake!' She angrily drove home the point that he seemed to have ignored completely. 'But did she care about me and what I was being subjected to? Did she hell!' The words scored across his steadily greying face. 'She was too busy screaming in hysterics while the rest of your damned guests were falling over each other to get into the room to see what was going on!'

He muttered something beneath his tight breath, but Annie didn't hear it; she was reliving her worst nightmare and it held her stiff and shaking.

'I was labelled a cheap little tramp before I left your apartment.' Her breasts heaved up and down on a forced breath. 'No one bothered asking me for my side of the story. They just saw what they wanted to see,' she said bitingly. 'A nice juicy scandal where supposedly sweet Angel Lacey of all people was caught red-handed with another woman's husband!' She shuddered, feeling sick. 'They saw what they wanted to see,' she repeated thickly.

'I'm—sorry,' César dropped grimly into the throbbing silence.

She didn't acknowledge him. 'All I wanted to do was try to forget the whole ugly episode,' she went on after a while. 'Then the next thing I know I'm being cited as the other woman in your sister's divorce and my name is being splattered all over the place! Who was going to believe my side of the story then, Mr DeSanquez?' she demanded bitterly. 'Two months after the event, who was going to believe that I was near-as-damn-it raped?'

His stark expression gave her the answer, and Annie grimaced bitterly. 'So the sweet Angel Lacey fell swiftly from grace,' she concluded, 'and I became the notorious Annie Lacey instead—fit to be used for anyone's convenience—including yours.'

He flinched; she accepted it as her due. 'Now, if you don't mind,' she said more calmly, 'I would like to leave here as soon as it's possible.' With that she turned to walk away.

But he stopped her, not by touch but with words. 'Susie,' he bit out grimly. 'Why does Susie not know about your true relationship with Hanson? They have lived together—shared the same bed for six months! Surely some kind of trust should have evolved in that time?'

'You would think so, wouldn't you?' Annie smiled a tight little smile. 'But then, she's always harboured an unnatural hatred of me. Now I know why, of course—' she shrugged '—her being connected with you lot.' It wasn't said nicely and wasn't meant to be. 'But in openly despising me she got Todd's back up.'

Slowly she turned to look coolly at him. 'You see, if any good came out of the Alvarez scandal, then it was the way it brought Todd and me much closer together. He believed my version, you see, Mr DeSanquez. Against all the evidence your family and so-called friends stacked against me, he believed me, stood by me and tried his best to shield me from the worst of the flak the Press wanted to throw at me.

'You could say we found each other,' she likened whimsically. 'And, in so doing, woe betide anyone who tries to come between us, because it will be at their peril— warn Susie,' she added as a mere mocking aside.

'You say you and Susie only share the eyes,' she went on. 'But you don't. You share ruthlessly manipulative natures too. Like you she was willing to go to any lengths to get what she wanted,' she explained, without acknowledging the sudden, angry flash in his eyes at that last insult. 'But the day she challenged Todd to choose between me and herself she lost him.

'He may love her,' she conceded, 'but he also despises her for trying that. Now, when I tell him about this little—charade she fixed up for me,' she pointed out, 'he'll cut her right out of his life. And don't take that statement lightly,' she warned when scepticism lightened his eyes, 'because just as you and Susie bear similar genes so does Todd to his father. He'll do it for my sake, just as his father did it to me for his wife's sake.'

'And you?' César questioned. 'Do you possess that same streak in you?'

Do I? Annie paused to think about it. 'I don't know,' she was forced to admit in the end. 'It hasn't been put to the test yet.'

'Then maybe it is time that it was,' he murmured. 'The way I hear you, Hanson means all the world to you. Will you—cut him right out of your life for his own sake?' he challenged silkily.

Annie frowned. 'I don't see the connection.'

He thrust his hands into the pockets of his loose-fitting trousers. 'I still hold the final card, Angelica,' he reminded her carefully. 'And, bearing in mind your analysis of my character just now, it will do you well to remember my ability to use it. Nothing has changed, except, maybe, my opinion of you as a person,' he allowed. 'But the success of *Cliché* still hangs on the promise of my collaboration.'

An icy shiver slid down Annie's spine. 'I still don't see what you're getting at,' she said warily.

His eyes were hard now, his expression grim. 'You either keep to your side of our deal,' he softly spelled out for her, 'or I will withdraw my support at the eleventh hour, giving Hanson no chance to put something else in my place.'

Annie took a stunned step back. 'You would still do that?' she choked. 'After everything I've just told you?'

His expression was bleak but firm. 'Susie needs time to mend her relationship with Hanson,' he stated grimly. 'I promised her that time. That promise cannot be forfeited simply because you have pointed out to me what I already knew—that my family can be quite ruthless when they need to be.' Narrowly his green gaze watched her. 'The rise or decline of Hanson Publications remains firmly in your hands, Angelica. You stay here with me and everything runs smoothly. You insist on leaving and it all falls the other way.'

'You bastard,' she breathed. He was no better than his thankless family! Like them he was prepared to sacrifice her feelings as if they didn't matter! 'Last night counts for nothing—nothing at all to you!'

His eyes seemed to go black, the green blanked out by an emotion that Annie was too hurt and angry to interpret. 'It counts,' he granted roughly. 'And indeed alters things slightly...' His pause was deliberate and chilling. 'I did not use protection last night, Angelica. And with hindsight I must presume that neither did you.'

Not slow at getting his meaning, she went so white that her eyes looked like huge dark pools in her horror-pinched face.

A nerve twitched in his jaw as he watched her, but his mouth remained firm with resolve. 'Which leaves us with another—problem we may yet have to face,' he went on. 'Which is whether you are pregnant with my child and, if you are, what we are going to do about it.'

It was all too much. Shock upon shock over the last twenty-four hours, plus the added emotional wrench of her own recent trauma in allowing herself to open up to this man, had Annie swaying, the beauty of the new day fading around its edges until it encompassed only his grimly watchful face.

Pregnant? She shook her head on a laugh that came very close to hysteria. No, she would not so much as allow herself to consider that as a possibility. Fate would not be that cruel to her, surely?

'It has to be acknowledged, Angelica,' he murmured, as though her thoughts were written across her face for his exclusive benefit. 'Children are not made in heaven, as I suspect you would prefer to believe. They are made by the ejaculation of male sperm into the female womb— a process we well and truly carried out last night.'

She flinched, his blunt, clinical description making her hands clutch at her stomach on a shudder of revulsion— an action that made a nerve twitch in his jaw again.

'So what are you asking of me now?' she demanded finally, the very quiver in her voice mirrored in the reactionary tremor of her body. 'Visitation rights when this other farce with Todd is over? Or perhaps you want even more than that,' she added bitterly, fingers lifting to comb her hair agitatedly away from her paste-white face. 'Maybe you prefer to rip the thing from my damned womb before it can cause any more trouble for you!'

At that it was his turn to flinch, but if she gained any satisfaction from it she wasn't aware. Her whole world seemed to have gone topsy-turvy, and she didn't know what she was feeling any more.

'Neither of those things,' he denied. 'I was, actually, about to suggest the *only* option I see open to us. Marriage,' he announced. 'I think you and I should get married, Angelica, and as soon as it can be arranged.'

CHAPTER SEVEN

HYSTERIA did take over now. Annie felt it rise like a lift out of a control from the very base of her feet until it burst free somewhere hot between the ears.

'I don't believe you're real!' she gasped out shrilly. 'I really don't believe you come from this planet at all!' Her blue eyes stared at him through a glaze of utter incredulity. 'I wouldn't marry you if you got down on your knees and begged me to!' she seared at him. 'I wouldn't even be standing here giving you this much of my time if you hadn't incarcerated me on this bloody island of yours!

'My God!' she choked, a hand flying haphazardly up in the air then landing bewilderedly on the top of her head. 'You're sick, do you know that? You ought to see a doctor—the kind who looks inside your head to see what the hell went wrong with it to make you what you are! Or, better still,' she rattled on furiously, 'refer him to me and I'll tell him exactly what's wrong with you, César DeSanquez! You are the result of too much interbreeding from your vengeful Spanish side, that's what you are!

'Marriage? Babies?' she shrieked. 'I would rather rip this hypothetical child out of my womb myself than be party to bringing another of your kind into this w—!'

The stinging slap issued to the side of her face silenced her. The hands suddenly gripping her shoulders and pulling her hard against him made her gasp. The eyes, when she managed to focus on them, were aflash with rage. He looked bigger, darker, more alien than he'd ever managed to look before. And he was throbbing with enough barely leashed violence to knock her down to the ground if she so much as provoked him a fraction of an inch further.

'You will take that back,' he breathed furiously. 'Every word of it. Every filthy, bitter word!'

'You go to hell,' she whispered, shaking with a wild combination of fear and fury.

'I am already there,' he rasped, and dropped his mouth down onto hers.

And she couldn't believe it but it was there—that strong and that quick!—a volcanic eruption of all those feelings that he had so brutally set free the night before!

With a whimpered groan of surrender she weakened at the knees, that tidal heat of wild pleasure sending her melting helplessly against him, jaw slackening, lips parting to allow him angry entry into her mouth.

When he stopped being angry and became aroused himself she wasn't sure. But the kiss did change, turning to something deep and intense, his tongue coiling sensually with her own while his hands slackened their grip enough to slide caressingly beneath her top, shrouding her in fine, pleasurable shivers as he stroked with excruciating lightness across her fine white skin.

She groaned again, her body arching instinctively, and he encouraged her with the deep, drugging urgency of his kiss. Then one hand was moving to her behind, splaying and pressing, drawing her into the braced arch of his thighs where the pulsing evidence of his arousal throbbed through the thin covering of her shorts, shocking and exciting her with the blatant power of his need.

Then suddenly he was breaking the kiss on a fierce intake of air, whistling it in through his teeth as he threw his dark head back in an effort to snatch back control, muttering tight words in Spanish to himself while his hands maintained that pressure against his pulsing thighs.

'No,' he gritted tensely while she waited, panting, frightened, weirdly excited by this effect that she seemed to have on him. 'No,' he said again, sounding hoarse with desperation, then lowered his head and opened his eyes.

They were eyes she found herself drowning in—eyes the same colour as the glittering jade water further out in the bay, eyes that yearned and hated and fought a battle that held her in absolute thrall.

'I will take you now, here on this rock in broad daylight, if I have to,' he enunciated rawly through the trauma of emotion running rife within him. 'And I will go on taking you until you agree to marry me, Angelica Lacey. Marry me and let me lock you away where you can never harm a child of mine. Do you understand?'

Understand? 'And how do you think your wonderful family would react to that?' she flashed bitterly back at him. 'Their gallant knight marrying the enemy!' She made a sound of scorn. 'My God, your sister would die at the horror of it and Susie would expire with chagrin!'

'And what do you think it will do to you if we do not marry?' he flashed right back. 'Or don't you care that carrying a child without a wedding ring will only help to confirm the notorious Annie Lacey's whoring ways?'

She went white, her hand snaking up to make vicious contact with his face—only it never made it. He caught her wrist in a manacle-like grip and held it suspended two inches from his cheek.

'They see what they want to see,' he quoted back at her quite ruthlessly. 'And they will see a woman who eats, sleeps and lives for sex. They will probably decide that you could not even give the father a name!'

'I could,' she spat at him. 'Yours! That wonderful genius Adamas, no less!'

'And the moment you use my name I will slap a court order on you demanding all rights to my child on the grounds that you are not a fit person to take care of it!' he vowed. 'Who do you think will win in a court of law, Angelica?' he challenged brutally. 'The whore or the genius with the blameless past?'

'My God—' She swallowed tensely on the hot ball of fury blocking her throat. 'Luis Alvarez has nothing on you, does he?'

That hit him on the raw, tightening that arrogant face until the tanned skin lay stretched taut across his lean cheeks. 'I want your agreement,' he bit out.

Annie gave a sound of angry bewilderment. 'There may not even be a child!' she cried. 'So why the hell are we having this crazy confrontation?'

'Because if there is,' he clipped, 'I want to be sure— damned sure—that no one will have cause to question its parentage. And with your track record—true or otherwise,' he put in at the bitter flash from her eyes, 'the poor child is destined to grow up being known only as Annie Lacey's bastard! Is that what you want?'

She flinched, sickened to her very depths because no matter how she tried to refute that insult she could not and knew she could not. Annie Lacey's reputation was set.

The tension she was maintaining in her captured wrist died along with the rest of her ability to fight, and her head lowered, the slow burn of wretched, self-contemptuous tears pressing against the backs of her eyes.

'We could at least wait a couple of weeks to find out if it's worth all of this grief!' she choked out wretchedly.

But he was already shaking his dark head. 'I want this child's hapless beginnings to be blameless, Angelica,' he stated grimly. 'And if that means us taking a risk and

marrying now then we will do it. For the child's sake,'
he punctuated forcefully. 'Not our own.'

'Oh, God. I hate you,' she whispered thickly. 'I hate
you so much!'

'But you now see the sense in what I am saying,' he
insisted. The hand still holding her wrist aloft tightened
its grip in a demand for the right reply.

She gave it anguishedly. 'Yes—yes!'

His big, bronzed chest, gleaming in the sunshine beneath the loose fall of his open shirt, lifted and fell. 'I
will arrange for us to be married tomorrow on Pelican
Island,' he decided, 'which is only a short flight away.
Then we will come back here until we know for sure
either way.' Slowly he lowered her wrist to her side and
released it.

'Then?' she prompted thickly. 'What then?'

He shrugged, his beautiful broad shoulders shifting
tensely beneath the thinnest cotton. 'That decision will
have to wait until we know the answer,' he said, then
turned and simply walked away.

The journey to Pelican Island was achieved in near
silence. Annie sat quietly beside César as he played the
controls, their sunglasses in place to protect their eyes
from the bright sun.

They had barely spoken a word to each other during
the last twenty-four hours. He hadn't been around to
talk to! Because a few minutes after he'd walked away
from her on the beach he'd left the island, bringing the
helicopter rising above the house then speeding off into
the clear blue sky.

He had returned late, just as the sun had been dying
out of a rich vermilion sky.

'It is all arranged,' he'd informed her when she'd
eventually forced herself to go downstairs and face him
over the dinner that Margarita had so carefully pre-

pared. 'We marry tomorrow afternoon on Pelican Island.'

'I thought Pelican Island was private,' she'd murmured, recognising the island's name as a famous retreat for the rich and stressed-out.

'It is leased,' he'd corrected, 'as my own island is. But because it possesses a hotel it is licensed to perform marriage services.'

Which had left her with nothing else to say. So they'd done their best to compliment Margarita's delicious dinner of goujons of chicken followed by freshly caught snapper fish on a bed of fluffy aromatic rice.

During his absence she'd explored Hook-nose Bay, scrambling over rocks and soft silver sand, swimming for hours in the calm waters. That evening her skin had borne the healthy glow of a day's unremitting sunshine—the high-factor lotion she'd found in the bathroom having protected her from the worst of the sun's rays.

By dinnertime she had been tired—tired enough not to care what he thought of her silence or the fact that, other than by that one short burst of conversation, she had barely acknowledged his presence.

He wanted all of this, not her. She needed to make no effort to pretend otherwise, and oddly he had seemed to accept that, his green gaze straying occasionally to her closed face but without attempting to intrude on the self-absorbed shell that she had withdrawn behind.

He waited until they were almost due to land before doing that. 'I have reserved a beach cottage for us at the hotel.' His shaded eyes glanced at her quietly composed features. 'I thought you might appreciate the—privacy until the ceremony is due to take place.'

She said nothing, but her fingers curled slightly in tense reaction where they rested on her lap.

'I have also arranged for something—appropriate for you to wear,' he added casually.

That brought her gaze to him. 'What I'm wearing is more than suitable,' she insisted, adding cynically, 'it isn't as though it's going to be the wedding of the year, after all.'

'I never implied it was,' he agreed almost soothingly. 'And you would look beautiful in whatever you chose to wear, be it sackcloth or that blue linen you have on now. But...' He paused to make a slight adjustment to their flight, his movements deft with confidence as he realigned the helicopter with the bulk of land that she could see looming towards them. 'This will not be a hole-and-corner wedding, Angelica,' he said grimly. 'It is important that it appears the happiest day in both our lives.'

Grin and bear it, in other words, she noted. Well, she was a professional, wasn't she? An absolute expert at make-believe? 'I won't let you down.'

'I know you won't,' he murmured quietly. But the tension between them was beginning to fizz again, and after a moment he sighed. 'Angelica, I want you to believe me when I say I mean you no harm! I do this for your own sake. Your reputation will not stand another scandal!' His eyes flicked to hers. 'I am sorry if that offends you, but it is the truth and I think that you know it!'

'Ah, I see.' The first bubbles of anger began to ferment in the calm interior she had been so carefully maintaining. 'So this is just another case of César DeSanquez being the gallant knight in action. How very altruistic of you,' she said waspishly. 'Remind me to thank you for it some time.'

'I don't look for your thanks,' he snapped, but from the way his lean profile clenched she knew that she'd managed to hit him on the raw. 'I am simply trying to tell you that you can trust me!'

'Trust?' She made a hard sound of scorn. 'Don't talk
to me about trust,' she derided. 'I will never trust another
human being again.'

No answer to that. Annie waited, seething in silence,
for him to pile the blame back on her, as he had so com-
petently done with everything else, but nothing came.
He just tightened his mouth and increased their speed,
and let the animosity that she was determinedly gener-
ating try its best to choke the very air around them.

They landed beside a row of low palm trees that
formed a line of shelter from the fiercest heat of the sun
along the inevitable crescent-shaped beach.

Annie waited patiently while César shut down the
engine then jumped down to come around and help her
alight. As they ran clear of the steadily slowing blades
Annie noticed the scattering of pretty, red-roofed
bungalows almost hidden from view amongst a rich
mixture of tropical shrubs and trees.

A man, tall and tanned and leanly built, met them
with a welcoming smile and a warm shake of their hands.
He was American, and older than he looked at first
glance. It was obvious that he knew César well because
after the initial introductions, and—she supposed—the
expected congratulations, he fell into warm conversation with César as he led them along a path towards
one of the bungalows.

Annie didn't bother to listen. She had, in fact, effectively switched off—something she had learned to do
early on in her career, when time had dragged heavily
during long, tedious waits between short, hurried shoots.

The inside of the bungalow revealed a surprisingly
large sitting room furnished in prettily covered rattan.
A pair of plate-glass sliding doors stood open on a view
that drew her attention, and she walked over to gaze out
at it while the two men finished their conversation.

Then a door closed quietly and there was silence behind her—the kind of silence that began to shred her nerve-ends as she tried to pick out just where César was without her having to turn to find out.

She felt a real reluctance to look him fully in the face. She hadn't done so, she realised—not voluntarily, anyway—since the night they'd shared a bed.

The chink of ice on glass told her that he was over by the little bar she had spied as she'd come in. And her nerves shredded a bit more when he came to stand directly behind her, a bronzed forearm lightly covered with silky, black hair appearing in her vision. He was holding a tall glass filled with something clear and refreshing, tiny bubbles swirling up from the chunks of ice settled at its base.

'Nothing too alcoholic,' he said. 'Mostly tonic, a splash of lime and the smallest tot of gin.'

'I don't drink spirits,' she informed him coolly, refusing to accept the glass.

'I have noticed,' he drawled, refusing to withdraw it. 'Another lesson taught by Alvarez?' he asked. 'I believe you were very drunk when you were seen being led into the bedroom that night.'

'Your bedroom,' she punctuated tightly.

'Yes.' He sighed. 'I'm sorry I ever said that but yes, it was mine.'

She swallowed on whatever was thickening her throat. His bedroom—his apartment. His bedroom—his island. It was as if he had to be connected with all the real traumas in her life.

'I sold the apartment, Angelica,' he inserted quietly. 'I never stepped foot in it again after that night. I could not cope with the vision of the woman I wanted for myself lying in the arms of another man. Any man,' he extended roughly. 'The fact that it happened to be

Alvarez only helped to generate my contempt of him—
not my contempt of you.'

'You can say that now, with hindsight.' She smiled
sceptically.

'It is the truth,' he stated. 'You were drunk. Everyone
who saw you allowed you that much at least. So did I.'

Yes, she had been drunk. Giddy, hiding all her hurts
from the world behind a screen of careless gaiety. 'I
suppose you are now making the assumption that, being
drunk, I probably encouraged him to do what he did.'
She didn't want it to, but her voice sounded husky with
hurt.

He sighed again, reaching around her with his other
hand so that his body had to make a glancing contact
with her own as he firmly took hold of her hand and
lifted it, pushing the glass into her palm.

'I am learning,' he murmured while she stood breathlessly cocooned in the circle of his arms, 'to make no
assumptions about you, Angelica. And no,' he added,
'I do not believe you encouraged him—because you tell
me it was not so. And, although you may not have
noticed, I have believed every word you've ever said to
me without needing corroboration. The truth, you see,
tends to glow like a challenge in your beautiful, defiant
eyes.

'So take the glass,' he urged. 'Drink to quench your
thirst, and maybe to steady your nerves a little for what
is to come.'

Her fingers tightened around the glass.

'Thank you,' he murmured, as though she had just
conceded some obscure but precious point, while Annie
had to fight a new battle with the tears that wanted to
fall from her eyes.

Then he was stepping back and she found that she
could breathe again, but the glass chattered against her
teeth as she lifted it to her quivering mouth.

'Now.' With distance between them, he sounded more like his normal, arrogant self. 'Over to your left there is an *en suite* bedroom set aside for your exclusive use. I have a matching one to your right. You have just under an hour, Angelica, to turn yourself into the beautiful bride I expect to see when I meet you back here.' With that he turned and walked away.

A beautiful bride.

Annie stared at herself in the full-length mirror and wanted to throw something at it to smash to smithereens the person she saw looking back at her.

Professional training gave her the expected bridal look, the equipment to do it having been provided by a man hell-bent, it seemed to her, on causing her everlasting pain.

The gown she'd found waiting for her was white, frothy, lacy, unashamedly romantic, with flamboyant off-the-shoulder sleeves edged with a deep ruffle of the finest hand-stitched lace—the same lace that floated around the low scooped neck of the fitted bodice and was sewn into the hem of its full, ballerina-length skirt.

The whole confection was about as far away from what anyone would expect Annie Lacey to wear for her wedding as a gown could get. Shy, frivolous, sweet— virginal.

And she felt a bigger fraud than ever.

A light tap at her door had her turning to face it just as César let himself into the room. Her breath caught on a silent gasp, her blue eyes darkening in surprise at how he looked.

He was dressed almost entirely in white himself. White trousers of the finest, finest cotton. White cotton over-shirt with a mandarin collar fastened from tanned throat to waist by what looked like sapphire studs—the genuine article, she assumed, knowing who he was. No tie—the shirt did not warrant a tie. It was as he turned slightly to close the door behind him that she saw the white silk ribbon holding his jet-black hair in place.

'The accepted dress of a Venezuelan,' he answered her curious look. 'It is called a *Liqui-Liqui*.'

Strange man, she found herself thinking achingly. An unconventional man. A man with such conflicting sides to his character that she found it impossible to work him out. Sometimes proud, coldly conventional, sometimes so avant-garde that he shocked her—like now.

My God, she thought hectically. He's really a complete stranger to me. And I'm about to marry him!

A shudder ran through her—of horror or fear or excitement she wasn't sure, because he had her so confused that she really could not be sure of anything any more.

He had come to a standstill one long stride into the room, his green gaze narrowed on her as it travelled slowly from the dainty white satin shoes on her feet to the top of her golden head. Annie waited in mute defiance for him to make some remark about the distinct lack of decoration on her head.

Sheer habit had made her dress her hair to suit the garment she was wearing; the long hair had been caught up in a silky twist at her crown, then she'd teased fine silken strands to fall around her face so that they accentuated the delicate line of her long, slender neck, but she'd drawn the line at adding the lace veil with its circlet of blue rosebuds—a crowning hypocrisy she refused to comply with.

'You look beautiful,' he said gruffly.

She didn't bother to answer. She was Annie Lacey, after all—professional model. She knew how good she looked.

So a short silence followed, one which oddly caught at the tiny muscles in her stomach and tied them into knots. This should not be happening, she told herself wretchedly. Neither of us wants it. None of it is real.

'Here.' He broke the silence, walking towards her with a flat velvet box in his hand.

Annie instantly recognised it for what it was, and snapped her hands behind her back. 'No, I won't wear whatever it is,' she refused.

'Why not?' A sleek black brow rose in question.

She gave a stubborn shake of her head. 'I don't need your jewels, Mr Adamas,' she used the name bitingly. 'Only your real name for appearance's sake.'

'Still fighting me, Annie?' He smiled. But it wasn't the teasing note in his voice that made her quiver, it was the use of her pet name falling for the first time from his beautifully sculptured lips that did it.

She struggled for breath. 'I think I've been remarkably compliant, if you must know,' she told him. 'But I draw the line at looking as if you bought me with—those.' Her eyes flicked a contemptuous glance at the unopened box. 'Keep them for your next wife,' she suggested tartly. 'Since this one is already praying for deliverance before the rest of this month is out.'

He should have got angry. She'd certainly intended provoking him into it. But he didn't; his green gaze studied her stiff face for a moment before he said quite gently, 'Five million dollars is a lot to pay for a wife, Angelica.' And as her mouth dropped open in stunned disbelief he tossed the velvet case onto the bed behind her. 'But I am willing to pay it for just one kiss from your *sweet* lips.'

She was still too busy struggling with the cost of whatever was in the box to realise his intentions. So when his mouth closed gently over her own she found herself returning the kiss without really being aware that she was doing it.

'You just earned your prize,' he murmured gruffly as he lifted his head. Then he added tauntingly, 'Or were you too busy counting dollar signs to notice?'

She blinked up at him, taking a moment or two to realise just what he was getting at. Then her blue eyes flared on a surge of anger and she spun around, lurching to grab at the velvet case then twisting to thrust it right back at the arrogant swine.

But he was already over by the door. 'Five minutes,' he warned. 'Wear them or not. I really do not care. They now belong to you.'

'But I don't want them!' she shouted at his disappearing back.

'And neither, *querida*, do I.'

She wore them in the end. Out of sheer cussedness or because she had the oddest feeling that she'd managed to offend him over the dratted things, she wasn't sure. But it was certainly with a grudging defiance that she eventually opened the box and found herself staring at the most beautiful necklace she had ever seen in her life.

Sapphires—exquisite dark blue sapphire hearts circled by tiny diamonds and linked together by the finest white gold, each setting a perfect match to the next—and the next and the next! There were over a dozen of them in all, fashioned to balance the larger central stone that quite literally took her breath away.

But that wasn't all. Nestled in the sensual curve of each sapphire heart sat a diamond—heart-shaped again, and seeming to flash a message at her that she refused to read. It had to be her imagination, she told herself breathlessly, because the white gold claw grips which held the two jewels together took on the shape of fingers to her mesmerised eyes, as though each pair of hearts rested in the palm of a delicate hand.

She couldn't wear these! She couldn't!

Yet, when a warning knock sounded at her door, she found herself tremulously fixing the necklace round her throat before she hurried from the room.

'Thank you,' he murmured when she eventually joined him, and once again she gained the impression that her compliance had actually managed to move him.

Feeling tense and nervous, she reacted with bad grace. 'Well,' she snapped, 'where is this charade supposed to take place?'

A small nerve twitched in the corner of his straight mouth. 'Here,' he answered quietly. 'Right here.' And indicated with an outstretched hand the open glass doors.

'Outside?' she questioned in surprise.

'It is traditional.' He nodded gravely.

A frisson of something frighteningly close to yearning shivered through her. No. She swallowed tensely. She couldn't go through with it. Not like this. Not with all the—

'Come, Angelica.' His hand closed gently around her slender waist.

'N-no,' she whispered. 'I can't do this. It isn't right. I feel a fraud. I...'

César turned her fully to face him, a hand coming up to cup her chin gently. 'Don't lose courage now,' he entreated softly. 'Everything will be fine, you'll see. Trust me.'

Trust him. He kept on telling her to trust him, but how could she when he had done nothing but trick and deceive her from the first moment they'd met?

'Please,' he murmured deeply, as if he could read her thoughts as his own. 'Please?'

His eyes held onto hers, dark green and probing, seeming to reach right inside her to some tiny, frightened point of need and soothe it gently. Her body quivered on a shaky little sigh, her mind going fluffy as it began to lose its grasp on reason.

A flash bulb popped.

'Are we ready?' a soft voice intruded.

Annie turned her head, seeing what her dazed mind interpreted as an angel standing in the open doorway to the room—a small, dark-skinned angel with snowy white hair, white flowing robes and a beautiful smile.

She blinked in an effort to clear her head, glanced hazily back at César, who had not moved his gaze from her face.

She felt trapped suddenly, lost, drowning in the compelling expression in his eyes. So much so that she didn't see the second flash bulb pop, did not even notice the photographer who was capturing in full Technicolour Annie Lacey decked out in white lace and sapphires, gazing into the eyes of the man she was about to marry.

CHAPTER EIGHT

IT WAS over. And the moment they found themselves alone again Annie seemed to lose complete grip on reality.

Strain, she told herself in some vague corner of her mind. You've cracked beneath the strain, and dropped weakly down into a nearby chair.

César had disappeared into his own room. He had murmured a reason for going at her but she hadn't absorbed the words. Her mind seemed to have completely shut down. Nothing going in—nothing much coming out. It was a strange, lost, floaty feeling that kind of buffeted her gently from the inside, holding her slack-limbed and still.

Coming back from his bedroom, César stopped dead, his gaze homing in on her frail white figure, looking more lost and vulnerable than he had seen her to date. A moment's anguish passed across his face, forcing his hands into two tense fists before he grimly relaxed them; then he was moving forwards to go and squat down beside her.

Carefully he reached for her hands. They were cold, and gently he began chafing them between his own. 'Surely it was not quite this bad an ordeal?' he mocked, infusing a teasing lightness into his tone.

She turned her head to look at him, her eyes like two huge sapphires in her lovely white face. 'Why the photographer?' she asked.

His shrug was careless. 'He came with the package,' he said. 'Why, did he bother you?'

'No.' Nothing bothered her. Not any more. She looked away again, her eyes drifting sightlessly back to the open windows where a soft, warm breeze disturbed the curtains pulled back by thickly plaited ties.

A knock came at the door; César laid her hands back on her lap before standing up and moving away. Annie looked down at them, stretching out the fingers where two new rings glinted in the light—one a hand-crafted, intricately woven band of the richest, purest gold, the other a beautiful sapphire and diamond ring designed to match the necklace at her throat. When César had slipped it on her finger directly after he had slid the gold band there she'd been too surprised to protest.

Now she just stared at it and wanted to weep.

A movement in front of her brought her unblinking gaze upwards. César was standing over her, a cup of something steaming hot in his hands. Silently he handed it to her. Annie caught the scent of a good old-fashioned cup of tea, and sipped gratefully at it until she felt life begin to return to her body at last.

'Thank you,' she murmured finally. 'That was thoughtful of you.' Then, because he was just standing there watching her with a concerned frown marring his attractive face, she added wryly, 'I'm sorry. I seemed to lose contact with myself for a few minutes there.'

'But you feel better now?'

'Yes.' She flexed one of her hands and watched the colour seep back into the bloodless skin. 'Odd—to have such a reaction to something that is, after all, only a sham.'

He didn't answer, something vaguely disturbing in his still, quiet stance. Then, before she could try to work out what was troubling him, he made a move that was rather like a gesture of contempt.

'You're right,' he agreed. 'The whole thing was an absolute farce. With hindsight I cannot think of a more flippant way to make such solemn vows.' He sounded harsh and bitter. Annie glanced at him in surprise, but he was already turning away. 'Take your time. Enjoy your tea,' he invited as he strode tightly towards his own room. 'Then get changed and we will get out of here. The quicker we can be alone, the quicker we can put all of this from our minds!'

'Regretting it already, César?' she drawled.

He stopped. 'Maybe,' he said grimly without turning around. 'Maybe I am regretting the whole damned thing!'

So, what did you expect? she mocked herself starkly as he shut himself away. Protests? Reassurance? Avowals of undying love? Tears spread across her vision but she blinked them angrily away.

You're beginning to believe your own press, she told herself angrily. Annie Lacey gets married so therefore she must be in love.

But you're not in love with him, are you? Are you?

And he is certainly not in love with you!

They had another row before leaving the bungalow, this particular one ending up with them both shouting because this time Annie was determined to win—no matter how scathing he became.

'Will you take them back?' she insisted, thrusting the velvet case into the rigid wall of his chest. They were both safely in the case—the necklace and the beautiful sapphire ring. 'I don't want them!'

'Well, neither do I,' he countered, refusing to take hold of it. 'They're yours. I gave them to you, and if there was an ounce of good manners in you you would accept them graciously as most women would do!'

'I am not *most women*,' she snapped, taking offence at even that basically innocent remark. 'I do not accept ridiculously expensive gifts—even from the man who was my first lover!' she flashed at him before he could flash the remark at her, and she was sure that he would have done—she could see the threat of it glinting in his angry green eyes. 'Or because he happens to be my first husband, come to that,' she added for good measure.

'And your last if you don't stop this!' he countered impatiently.

'But why do you want me to have them?' she cried in honest, angry bewilderment. 'Why—why—why?'

To her absolute surprise dark colour spread across his high cheeks, a sudden discomfited look forcing him to hood his eyes. 'I made them for you,' he muttered, so gruffly that she barely caught the words.

'What?' she prompted doubtfully. 'What did you say? You made them—for me? Is that what you said?'

'Yes,' he hissed, as though the confirmation were wrenched forcibly from him. 'They were designed for you—made—made exclusively for you, OK?'

For the first time he sounded truly American. Usually he sounded a rather attractive mix of two cultures, but that forced admission, with its accompanying flail of one angry, defensive, very threatening hand that was warning her not to push the subject further, had been pure American bullishness all the way through.

She blinked, silenced. And with a harsh sigh he thrust his fists into the pockets of his casual camel-coloured trousers. 'If you don't want them,' he gritted, 'then sell them, chuck them—give them away. But don't try giving them back to me because I just don't want them.'

'But this is crazy!' she whispered when eventually she found her voice again, unable to leave the subject even with the threat he had issued still pulsing in the air between them. 'Why should you design something as beautiful as these for someone like me?'

Another sigh. His shoulders hunched, and for a long, tense moment Annie thought that he was going to refuse to answer. 'They match the colour of your eyes,' he said at last, in a tight dismissive tone that was supposed to make her say, Oh! That's why! with relief, when he had to know that that excuse had to be the most laughable he could have offered. These beautiful pieces had been conceived and made long before he'd ever met her, at a time when he'd despised her for everything she was.

'No,' she said. 'It isn't enough that the sapphires happen to match my eyes. Half the world's population has blue eyes! So you're either trying to fob me off with just about the weakest excuse you've come up with for anything to date or this is what I suspected it to be from the beginning—a gift of conscience. And, as such, I refuse to accept it—unequivocally.'

Their eyes locked on each other's, hers in challenge, his in a kind of defiance that she found strangely exhilarating. But as they continued to stand there warring silently other elements began to join in the battle. Her senses began to stir, tiny muscles deep down inside her beginning to pump to a rhythm that set her whole body pulsing.

He had to be feeling it too, because she watched his green eyes darken, his mouth slacken from angry tension into a heart-contracting sensuality.

No. She denied it as the air around them seemed to grow hot and heavy, the ability to breathe it in more difficult with each shallow breath. No. But she couldn't seem to find the will to break the disturbing contact.

Sex—she named it contemptuously as the whole cacophony of sensation grew into a pounding throb. He wants me, and, God help me, I'm responding! Fingers tingled with the need to touch; breasts stung with a need to feel his mouth closed around them. Warmth flooded the sweet, burning liquid of desire into her shaking limbs.

No. She denied it again. No! And in an act of sheer desperation she broke the mood by stretching out an arm and with a defiant sideways flick sent the velvet case slewing onto a nearby table.

It landed with a thud and a slither. César did not so much as bat an eyelid, but at least the hunger died out of his eyes.

He turned abruptly, placing his tense back with its ridiculous pony-tail towards her, and—damn it—she suddenly wanted to grab hold of that lock of hair, wrench at it, hurt him, launch herself at him and beat her fists against the ungiving wall of his back in an effort to relieve this—this crazy sense of bitter frustration throbbing in her blood!

Sexual frustration! she told herself angrily. And it's all his fault! He's done this to me! Made me aware, know, want—desire!

'Shall we go, then?' he said, and moved arrogantly off towards the door.

Instantly the feelings running rife inside her flipped over to become something else entirely, her gaze flicking to the discarded jewel-case then back to him again.

He didn't mean it, she told herself nervously. He was calling her bluff. No man just walked away and left what amounted to a five-million-dollar tip for the maid!

He was standing by the bungalow door with his hand curled around the handle, waiting for her to join him. Mutinously Annie walked forward, cold sweat beginning to trickle down her spine the closer she got to him, and still he made no move to retrieve the case. Unable to stop herself, she glanced back at it, black velvet askew on a polished tabletop. Her mouth was dry, her fingers twitching at her sides as she turned back to him.

'Don't,' she pleaded.

'Your choice,' he returned with ruthless indifference. And he calmly opened the door and stepped through it.

Annie hovered between a stubborn desire to defy him to the last and a real horror of what it would mean if neither gave in. Then with a growl of angry defeat she darted back to pick up the case.

Her eyes were hard as she walked back to him. To be fair, César made no remark whatsoever—either by word or gesture. He simply waited until she was out of the room then drew the door shut, his manner grimly aloof as he led the way back through the garden to the waiting helicopter.

It did not augur well for the journey back to his island. Annie was too busy drowning in a sea of her own resentment, and he seemed to have drawn himself behind a wall of impenetrable calm.

Still clutching the case, the moment they were back at the villa she made a bid for escape, stalking off towards the stairs with her spine and shoulders stiff.

'Annie.'

Her spine stiffened even more. For some unknown reason he had suddenly taken to calling her Annie, instead of Angelica in that crisp, tight way he used to use. She didn't like it. Didn't like what it did to her. It hinted at care and affection—an intimacy that touched tender places inside.

'What?' she bit out ungraciously, pausing but refusing to turn. If he had something to say then she was determined that he was going to say it to her back!

'Come swimming with me.'

Of all the things she might have expected him to say at that point that had never been in the running! The invitation stunned her—and the way he'd said it, with such wary uncertainty, shook her poise enough to make her spin around.

He was standing framed by sunlight in the open door, filling it, consuming the light so that she could not see his face. She slid her fingers absently over the velvet case while she tried to search out the catch in the invitation. He remained silent, watching her, waiting, tense—she could sense his tension even with the full length of the huge hall between them.

'Why?' she demanded finally.

'The bay has some wondrous sights to offer,' he answered quietly. 'I think you would enjoy discovering them with me.'

'I could make those discoveries just as pleasurably on my own,' she pointed out churlishly. 'Especially when you think I have two whole weeks to do little else but explore the bay.'

'But to do it with someone who knows it well will be much more rewarding,' he pointed out. 'And I would— enjoy sharing the experience with you.'

She was tempted; despite all the animosity darting around them she had to admit that she was tempted. It was hot, and she was fed-up, restless, eager to be using up some of the energy pounding like a frustrated rubber ball inside her. But swim with him? Display yet another climb-down from frosty aloofness to him?

'All right,' she heard herself say reluctantly, yet felt better for saying it, some of the tension easing out of her achingly taut frame. Then with a flash of inspiration she added slyly, 'I'll come if you'll relieve me of these.' Challengingly she held out the velvet case. 'I'll never get a moment's rest worrying about them otherwise. Lock them away in a safe or something—I presume you do have a safe here, considering who and what you are?'

Surprisingly he nodded, moving into action, that lean, muscled body sheer poetry in motion as he covered the distance between them. Without a word he took the case from her. With his face in the same shade she occupied she could now read his expression. Ruefully conceding seemed to describe it best.

He was giving her back what she had just given him— a climb-down. It helped to warm her frozen feelings a little.

'I will promise to guard them well for you.'

Not so big a climb-down, Annie acknowledged. But now she'd relaxed she couldn't seem to find the strength to start battling once again.

'Ten minutes?' he asked, seeming suddenly vitally alive as he walked off towards a door to the right of the vast hallway. 'On the beach,' he added. 'I'll bring the snorkelling gear.'

He was already waiting for her when she walked down from the house towards the small, sandy beach. He was dressed in nothing more than a pair of black swimming shorts, and her eyes flickered reluctantly over his long, tanned legs with their coating of crisp, dark hair that curled all the way up to the bulging apex at his thighs.

She swallowed, feeling that warm rush of awareness explode inside her. For a few dragging moments it held her helpless and distraught. Then she managed to close her eyes, shut out the pulsing cry of her awakened body, shut out the sight of the man who had incited it all to life.

'Ready?'

He sounded strange, as though something was constricting his throat. Glancing at him again, she felt a fine sweat break out on her skin at the expression on his dark, chiselled features as his eyes ran over her skimpy sugar-pink one-piece then came burning back to her face.

He knew. He knew why she had stopped walking and what was happening to her. He knew because she could see that the same thing was happening to him.

And it's getting worse, she accepted starkly. Stronger.

He looked away with a sharp, jerky gesture of denial, his solid jaw tightening, his big chest heaving, his hands clenching into two tight fists at his sides. Then he seemed to get a hold of himself. 'I thought we would borrow Pedro's boat,' he said. 'He keeps it in the next bay.' A hand lifted to indicate across the headland covered in lush tropical undergrowth. 'We can take it out and anchor it over the reef. That way we will see more.'

He didn't wait for an answer but bent to snatch up the snorkelling gear piled by his feet and strode off, back rigid, that black silky tail of hair covering the tension in his spine.

Her own inclination was to turn and run in the opposite direction. But, shaken and disturbed as she was by the power of need he had awoken inside her, she was also tensely aware that his needs were just as strong, and she had a horrible suspicion that if she did turn and run he would follow, and, as sure as hell, the eruption she could feel building steadily between them would happen. She could feel its threat to her bubbling fretfully beneath the thin surface of her self-control.

So she began to follow him, reluctant but aware that at least this way they both had time to pull themselves together.

She was right—well, half right—she noted wryly several tense minutes later as they emerged from a narrow pathway that led over the top of the rocky headland and through the lush undergrowth to a tiny circle of sand, where she could see a small boat with an outboard motor lying lopsidedly just above the tide line.

They were fine so long as they did not make eye contact with each other. And the fact that César was of the same mind made it easier to remain calm as he threw the snorkelling gear into the bottom of the boat then began dragging it, his muscles rippling in the sunlight, into the water before inviting her to get in.

'Pedro uses this for fishing,' he explained, once the motor had sprung into life and they were moving slowly across the top of the clear, calm sea. 'He catches something fresh and different every day.'

'They live very quietly here,' Annie remarked, her eyes fixed on the cut and swell of water around the boat.

'Don't they get lonely with no other company than their own?'

'They visit their family on the mainland quite often,' he told her. 'I have a launch anchored at Union Island. It is at their disposal whenever they feel the need to make use of it.'

'But no phone.' Annie frowned. 'How do they let anyone know what they want without some line of communication?'

'Been searching for a way to cry for help, Angelica?' he drawled.

Her cheeks flushed, because that was exactly what she had done yesterday after he'd left her alone. She'd wanted to ring Lissa—not Todd but Lissa—and beg her to find a way out of this mess without involving Todd.

Todd. Even white teeth buried themselves anxiously into her lower lip. If Todd found out what had been going on here there would be hell to pay. She was sure of it.

'There is a radio,' César inserted smoothly, 'linked directly with my head office in Caracas. But, other than that, they are, I assure you, content with their lot or they would not stay.'

'What kind of office?' she asked him, reluctantly curious about this man she had married. 'I mean,' she continued mockingly, 'what do you do when you're not being Adamas?'

He smiled at the way she had put that last bit. 'Actually, my fascination for precious stones and metal is really just a hobby.' He shrugged, as though a billion-dollar hobby was peanuts to him.

'But as DeSanquez—' wryly he used that mockery she'd used on himself '—I head the DeSanquez Organisation—oil, a couple of diamond and gold mines, a beef ranch or two, several other business interests which bring in a good revenue. All this I inherited from my father,' he informed her. 'But my mother was the family artist. From her I learned to develop my skill with precious metal and stones. From my father I learned to succeed in big business.'

The double persona. Annie had always known it was there in him. 'And the hair?' she asked, because it was the hair that first had made her suspect that he was two people. 'Do you wear it so long because of some DeSanquez tradition? Or—?'

His laughter was warm and resonant, and it shimmered through Annie like a heatwave. 'Nothing so—romantic,' he replied, still smiling. 'I simply—like it this way. Call it the artist in me, if you like, needing to make a stand against the businessman.' he cocked a quizzical eyebrow at her. 'Does it bother you?' he asked curiously. 'Would you rather I had my hair cut in a more conventional style?'

'No!' she denied impulsively, then flushed as his green eyes began to gleam. 'It—it doesn't bother me one way or the other,' she said offhandedly.

'Doesn't it?' he murmured softly. And she had to look away from those dark, knowing eyes, wishing that she hadn't mentioned his ridiculous hair!

She went quiet after that. And César turned his attention to guiding the little boat out of the shelter of the tiny cove and towards the mouth of Hook-nose Bay, where he stopped the engine and tossed the small anchor out onto the reef.

'Have you snorkelled before?' he asked.

Annie nodded and so did he. 'Good. So you know what to do with these.' He handed her a pair of flippers and a snorkelling mask. 'Give me a minute to get into the water and I'll help you out of the boat.'

Surprisingly it turned out to be an enjoyable hour. With César leading the way they snorkelled over the tip of and between narrow canyons of coral, treading water regularly when one or the other saw something interesting beneath them.

They saw brightly coloured cardinals and butterfly fish and spotted drums. Pretty blue parrot-fish swam in and out of the coral, and a couple of big groupers hurried away when they saw them coming. At one point César grabbed urgently at her hand, demanding her attention then pointing over to a deeper point on the coral where she could see a long, sleek silver fish with a pike-like face. Barracuda! she recognised instantly, and tried to turn and swim back to the boat.

But César stopped her, holding onto her arm and grinning at her through his mask. Firmly he pulled her off in the other direction, where they found an octopus sitting on a rock, his bulbous body swaying to and fro in the lazy current.

Then a dark brown moray eel slid its ugly face out from between two rocks and Annie decided with a shudder that she'd had enough. She turned swiftly before César could stop her and swam quickly back to the boat.

'Yuk!' she exclaimed as they both bobbed up beside the boat. 'Did you see that moray? He has to be about the ugliest creature alive in the sea!'

'Don't let Mrs Moray hear you saying that,' César warned teasingly. 'She may take offence and bite off your toes.'

The fact that Annie had just removed her flippers and thrown them into the bottom of the boat, leaving her toes very vulnerable, meant that his remark was well timed. She shrieked, and made a lurching dive for safety, almost managing to drown them both as she landed in a flail of arms and legs against his big, strong chest.

One of his arms closed instinctively round her while the other hand grabbed at the side of the boat, his amused laughter filling the air.

Then he wasn't laughing, and Annie had gone perfectly still because it had happened, just like that. Quick, strong and undeniable. Awareness—hot and stifling. Skin sliding wetly against skin. Bodies remembering—recognising the pleasurable potency of the other.

His arm was tight around her slender waist, his eyes burning fiercely into the wide, shocked depths of hers.

'Please, César, no,' she pleaded when she saw his gaze drop to her mouth.

'Why not?' he murmured huskily. 'Why not, when you know it is what we both want?'

'No.' She shook her wet head, fingers curling tensely into the rigid muscles in his shoulders.

'A kiss. Just a kiss.'

'No.' But she felt the muscles deep in her body tighten in sweet expectancy.

'Yes,' he countered, his eyes darkening languorously, his mouth taking on a soft, sensual curve. 'Yes, dammit, yes.' And he moved to angle his lips against her own.

Annie shied away, twisting her head and stretching her body as she made a desperate grab for the boat with both hands. The action set the little boat rocking precariously, and for a moment she hung there helplessly, because César did not immediately concede defeat and let her go, his arm remaining a possessive clamp around her slender waist. Her heart began to pump, tension in the muscles around it making each heavy thump painful. She closed her eyes, wet lashes spiked and trembling against the soft skin covering her high cheek-bones.

If he pulls me back...she thought tensely. If he pulls me back I'll give in to him. I know I will!

Then the arm was slackening, and instead of imprisoning it became two hands on her waist, helping to lever her into the boat.

She didn't look at him as he joined her there, and though she felt his eyes on her she let the tense silence grow. The afternoon was spoiled now anyway, the brief period of easy pleasure they had found in each other's company ruined by a torment that simply refused to go away.

César must have been thinking along similar lines, because instead of getting them under way he sat back and let loose a heavy sigh. 'Refusing to acknowledge it will not make it easier,' he said gravely. 'It simply makes it worse. Believe me, I know.'

'The voice of experience?' she flashed at him bitterly.

He grimaced then shrugged. 'Yes,' he admitted, though she suspected that he didn't want to.

'You are a complete stranger to me.' Grimly she stared at the gold band encircling her finger. 'A week ago I didn't know of your existence. Three days ago we met and parted without my even learning your name. Forty-eight hours ago...' Almost exactly, she then added as a bitter, silent adjoiner as her gaze drifted out to the steadily dying day. 'You were throwing insults and threats at me and vowing to ruin my life!'

'And two hours after that you were lying in my arms,' he added, 'getting to know me as intimately as a woman can. What does that tell you, Annie,' he prompted gently, 'about the insults and threats that preceded the passion?'

It told her that they were a front to what had really been erupting between them. Memories crowded in— hot, turbulent memories that darkened her eyes and thickened her breath. Then came the shudder of shame— the shame of knowing how easily and thoroughly she had surrendered to the morass of desires raging through her that night.

'Instant physical attraction is not uncommon between the sexes, Angelica,' César inserted quietly. 'It happens all the time.'

Not to me it doesn't, she thought. 'You are still a stranger,' she said. 'A man who set out to trap and manipulate me from the first moment we met.'

'I'm sorry.' He heaved an impatient sigh. 'I have learned to regret my original intentions. What else can I say?' His green eyes glinted at her in helpless appeal.

'Nothing,' she mumbled, and made a play of straightening the wet snorkelling gear littering the bottom of the boat.

César watched her for a while, his face tight and grim. Then he sighed again, and turned his attention to pulling up the anchor.

They chugged back to the little cove in sober silence, sitting close in the tight confines of the small boat, yet with a thick wall erected between them. With a deft cut of the motor at just the right moment he eased the nose of the boat up onto the beach on the crest of an incoming wave. Then he was jumping out and wading forwards to help Annie clamber out.

The feel of his hand on her arm made her flesh tingle, and she couldn't stop the revealing shiver that feathered her slender frame.

His grip tightened fractionally in response. 'It won't go away,' he repeated roughly from just behind her. 'We've lit the flame, Annie. Now it's hungry for more.'

She didn't answer, but pulled free of him and walked away on legs weak and trembling in reaction, because she knew that he was right. And, far from going away, it was getting stronger. Worse. Desperate almost.

Dinner that evening was an ordeal. To be fair to César he tried to keep the mood light and casual, but she could hardly look at him without feeling her senses catch light.

It frightened her—the intensity of her awareness of him. Her mind refused to stop replaying to her how his silken, tight skin, hidden beneath the conventional white shirt he was wearing, felt to the touch, or reminding her how those long, blunt-ended fingers he used to pick up his glass or lift his fork to his mouth could draw such clamorous pleasure from her. His mouth, sipping intermittently at wine, was saying words she did not hear, because she was too lost in the memory of how they had felt tasting her—

'More wine?'

'What?' She started, her eyes focusing on the sardonic expression in his. He knew, and she flushed, looking quickly down and away. 'No—thank you,' she refused, and jerked to her feet. 'I'm—t-tired,' she stammered nervously. 'I think I'll go to bed.'

She didn't wait for him to answer, didn't look at him again, but she was fiercely aware of his sardonic gaze following her hurried journey across the room, and felt as if she was ready to crack in two under the tension inside her as she left him with a flurry of nervous limbs.

CHAPTER NINE

THE moon set early in the Caribbean, leaving it to the myriad stars hanging in the satin-dark sky to provide what light there was filtering into Annie's bedroom. It was enough, or at least enough to save the room from a total blackout. She could just make out the mirror hanging on the opposite wall, for instance, and the dark shapes of furniture scattered about the room.

Wide awake, even though it had to be way past midnight, she traced the shapes lazily with her eyes, her body very still beneath the white cotton sheet that she had drawn up beneath her arms. But inside she was restless, troubled—disturbed by what was bothering her and what she could not seem to control unless she lay very still like this and breathed very carefully, and centred her whole concentration on keeping it all severely banked down.

Is this what it feels like, she wondered, to want what you shouldn't want? To desire what you should not desire? To need it so badly that it actually became the driving force for your life's blood?

Sighing shakily, she lifted a hand to rest it beneath her cool cheek, settling against it as though it would offer some comfort, some relief.

It didn't, and the fingers on the other hand began to tap a restless dance against the graceful curve of her long thigh beneath the sheet. Her gaze lowered to watch them, her mind acknowledging that the restlessness was beginning to break out. Perhaps she should get up and take a walk along the beach? she mused. Do something—anything to take her mind off what she knew was trying to break through all her restraints.

Sex. You've tasted the elixir, Annie, and now you're hungry for more.

She smiled at her own mockery, then stopped smiling, the fingers stopping their tapping when her gaze caught the washed-out glint of gold encircling the third finger on her left hand.

Married to a man who made you a millionairess within minutes of putting that ring there. She frowned. What had made him do it? No man in his right mind gave a woman he hardly knew a gift like that!

There again, no man who saw that woman as little better than a whore took her to bed and ravished her. Not a man of César's calibre, anyway.

He was a strange man—a complicated man. A man who contrarily confused, infuriated and fascinated her with his quick-fire changes in character. One minute arrogant, insufferably domineering—bullish. The next, soft, caring, gentle, considerate—dynamically charming when she least expected it.

Dangerous too, she added to her growing list. Dangerous because he had managed to do what no man before him had ever done, and had got beneath the protective skin she wore so thickly around herself. Dangerous because he wanted her with a hunger that burned constantly behind whatever else they were doing, whether that was slinging insults at each other or just trying—trying—to be civilised towards each other.

And what about yourself? she then countered grimly. Your behaviour is no less contrary than his! You profess to hate and despise him for what he's done, but you also want him with the same unforgivable hunger.

Every time you look at him you torture yourself with memories of how his lips felt against your own, or how frighteningly superb he looked naked and aroused, or what it felt like to have him deep inside you! If he so much as touches you your skin leaps into vibrant, burning life, your stomach muscles knot and your thighs throb.

Hell, even lying here just thinking of him and it's all beginning to happen!

Restlessly she moved again, flipping over to lie curled on her side, half considering getting up, going for that walk along the beach that she had suggested to herself, when her bedroom door came open, and all thoughts of any kind were suspended as the disturbingly dark bulk of a man seemed to fill the whole room.

He paused for a moment. She stopped breathing, her very bones tingling as if they'd just received an electric shock.

Then he was stepping inwards and closing the door behind him. Her heart took up an unsteady hammer. Eyes huge, throat locking, she watched him walk slowly towards the bed where she lay.

He was wearing a thin black cotton robe and nothing else as far as she could tell. And she could almost feel the tension in his body as he came closer, bringing with him the scent of male heat and the tantalising freshness of a spicy male soap.

As he came to a standstill right beside where she lay she lifted her eyes to let them clash with his; hers were wary, questioning what this unexpected visit meant when really she knew exactly what it meant. The reality of it was already turning the very tissue of her being to a warm, sensual liquid because his eyes were hiding nothing—nothing.

Yet in silence he waited. Breathlessly she waited. Eyes locked. The tension between them was so fraught that she could almost taste it, even ran her tongue around parched lips as if to do just that.

When long moments passed and she had said not a word he bent down towards her, braced his hands on the pillow either side of her head and murmured softly, 'Invite me to stay.'

Her senses quivered. 'I...' The sound came out frail and breathless—hardly a sound at all really as she found herself caught by the beauty of his sensually moulded mouth hovering a bare inch away from her own.

'Please.' He closed the gap and kissed her. It was nothing more than the gentlest touch of his mouth against her own, but her own lips clung as he drew away again.

'Please,' he repeated softly. 'Please...'

At last she breathed, her breasts lifting and falling on the small, constricted action. But other than that she couldn't manage another single thing. Yet...

Had she answered? she found herself wondering dizzily. She was vaguely certain that she hadn't said yes, but was also sure that she hadn't said no.

But whatever she did do César took it as an affirmative, because after a moment he whispered, 'Thank you.' Then he was straightening again, holding her gaze with his own darkly burning one as he unknotted and stripped off his robe, paused for a moment as if to give her a final opportunity to make a protest, jaw clenched, the rigid walls of his stomach clenched, his body already wearing the evidence of desire.

Then he lifted the edge of the thin sheet and in one fluid, graceful movement came to lie down beside her.

His fingers were trembling a little as he gently stroked them across her cheek and slid them beneath the heavy fall of her hair. Then he was drawing her towards him, turning her, moulding her, and slowly—oh, so slowly that her senses began to vibrate, her lips to pulse, part, gasp out a single shaky breath—he closed the gap between their mouths.

His lips were as full and pulsing as her own, both so hot that they seemed to fuse, the shock of it sending one of her hands jerking up to press against his chest.

He shuddered. It ran through him like a tidal wave, drawing a groan from him; then he was pushing her gently onto her back and coming with her, his upper body crushing her into the soft mattress as it pressed lightly down.

For a moment her courage failed, memories of that other hot violent eruption of passion making her gasp in shaky fear.

But he soothed her with a caressing hand. 'No,' he murmured, as if he knew exactly what had frightened her. 'This is passion I am feeling for you, not angry desire. It runs through my blood like a fire, but it is not destructive. Some fires cleanse, Angelica,' he told her softly. 'I want to cleanse that other experience from your mind.'

Then he was kissing her again, and any hope of forming a conscious decision for herself was lost in the slow, deep sensuality of it.

It went on and on, not even breaking when he began to caress her, his hand sliding against the smooth silk of her nightdress in a long, sweeping motion that followed the delicacy of her ribcage, the flatness of her stomach and finally the length of her thighs where the nightdress ended and satin-smooth flesh began.

She must have moved restlessly because he instantly soothed her again, bringing his other hand out from beneath her head to lay it gently against her cheek.

And still the beautiful kiss did not break. Nor did it when he spent an age seemingly content to stroke her like that. He didn't touch her intimately, didn't even try to remove her nightdress, but simply played a kind of magic with her flesh, coaxing, gently coaxing the fine, light tremors to overtake her, and eventually her muscles to begin expanding and contracting to the sensual rhythm he induced.

In the end she couldn't stand it, and dragged her mouth away from his with a sharp, helpless gasp for air. He let her go, his eyes almost sombre as they studied her, his hand pausing against the quivering flesh of her stomach.

'What?' he whispered. 'What?'

She closed her eyes in confusion. Even his softly spoken voice was having the most overwhelming effect on her. 'I don't know,' she breathed, panting a little in an effort to control what was happening inside her.

'Then don't try to think,' he advised. 'Just follow me. Trust me, Annie. And between us we will make this the most beautiful experience of our lives.'

Trust him. Follow him. She really did not have any choice. From the moment his mouth captured hers again she was lost—lost in the dark, sensual beauty of the man. Lost in what he could make her feel, and lost in the wonder of what she could do to him.

It was slow and it was rich and it went very deep, each touch, each caress, each accidental brush of their skin heightening an awareness inside them that seemed to encapsulate the two of them in a hot, dark world of their own.

His touch became more intimate, knowing, sending her boneless so she lay there in helpless thrall. The caress of his tongue on her eager skin drew soft gasps of pleasure from her, the silk-like thrust of his throbbing manhood nudging against her thigh filling her with a sense of power that made her bold.

When she began caressing him he fell heavily onto his back, to lie blatant in his desire for more, eyes closed, mouth parted, his gasps of pleasure urging her on. His skin felt like tightly padded satin, the muscles beneath it rigid then rippling in response to her touch. She kissed his damp throat then his shoulder, then, unable to resist it, tasted his sweat on her tongue, trailing it over his chest until she found and began to suck on his tight male nipple.

His hands jerked up to grasp her head tightly, holding her there while he seemed to stop breathing, to go motionless as the sensations she was causing inside him took hold.

Then her hand glided tentatively over his stomach, and he jolted into life like a man shot, startling her as he reared upwards and over her, his hand whipping down to imprison hers as his husky growl revealed the extent of his arousal before he was kissing her hungrily again, stopping her from thinking again, taking control again, slowing things down, drawing it out until she really believed that she was going to die if he didn't do something to ease the unbearable pressure building deep down inside her.

Her hand jerked to his hair, fingers curling, tightening, tugging with unknown violence, dragging the thin ribbon free so that the black satiny mass slid like a curtain all around her. She sighed against his mouth, restlessly urgent. Someone was groaning and whimpering, and she knew that someone was herself. Her senses were in ferment, rushing in a panicked stampede through her body in an effort to crowd where the tension grew.

He must have understood because he moved then, sliding between her thighs where his fingers still played their magic, keeping up that sensual rhythm until the very moment when he joined them in a single mind-blowing thrust.

Annie arched like a bow, arms flying out and upwards in total abandonment. He arched too, like a giant wolf about to howl its mournful song, his long back, his dark head in a taut arch of pleasure, and for a space out of time neither were of this earth, neither aware of the other as sensation washed their brains of all else.

Then she felt the tug of her own muscles, felt them draw him in deeper, felt him grow and throb and fill her; then desperate fingers were reaching for him even as he came down towards her.

Afterwards she lay wrapped tightly in his arms, his body curled round her as though she were in need of protection and he was determined to give it. They didn't speak, hadn't found the words to cover what had just taken place. All Annie knew was that in the moment when he'd entered her César had become her; she'd felt that right down to the very roots of her being. Whether he'd experienced the same thing she didn't know, but by the way he'd held her and kept on holding her, even long after he had fallen into a deep sleep, she had to believe that he had.

He woke her once more before morning, bringing her swimming up from sleep to the pleasure of his suckling lazily on one of her breasts. His caresses were already wreaking their magic on her body, filling her with a sweet, moist heat that made her stretch sensuously then sink on a shivery sigh into the rapture he was creating.

It was slow and it was relaxed and it was sleepy, and it seemed to draw a much deeper response from both of them which left them clinging to each other in a lead-weighted aftermath filled with nothing but a silent awe.

The next morning she awoke to find him still sleeping beside her, the sheet pushed down low over his thighs. He was lying on his side and facing her, an arm thrown heavily across her waist, his hair flowing over one satiny bronze shoulder, lying almost lovingly in that warm, moist hollow that formed the muscular ridge of his neck.

He looked different in sleep—more relaxed, more attractive while those sharp green eyes were hidden from view. His mouth still had that fatally sensual shape to it, but then, she acknowledged, it always did—whether he was tense or angry or just behaving normally. It was his mouth that had first ignited her senses and it had been wreaking its devastation ever since.

Feeling the stirring of excitement take root inside her at this near voyeuristic pleasure she was taking in just looking at him, she blushed and looked away.

Moving carefully so that she would not waken him, she slid out from beneath his arm and moved stealthily up and off the bed. Her body was stiff and aching, and she smiled wryly to herself as she made her way to the bathroom. They said sex was the best exercise for toning the body. She believed it. She felt as though she'd spent last night tied to a toning bed, except—a shiver of something incredibly sexy quivered through her—no toning bed left your senses feeling like this!

The shower was warm and refreshing, and she stood beneath it with her head tilted back, eyes closed while the water gushed over breasts still full and aching. Her nipples were tight and sharply sensitive, and seemed to have forgotten how to retract. She released a soft sigh as the water began to soothe them, though the ache between her thighs remained a dull, pulsing throb.

Was it always like this after a long night of loving? she wondered. This acute awareness of her own femininity? And was this strange yet pleasant feeling that she had been totally invaded all part of the allure that kept the desire to experience it again and again so strong?

'Good morning. You started without me, I see.'

The sound of that deep, pleasant voice accompanied a pair of long-fingered hands sliding around her wet ribcage.

She let out a startled gasp, her eyes flicking open as a warm mouth bent to nuzzle that susceptible point between her shoulder and throat. Her hands snapped up to cover his where they rested just beneath the heavy swell of her breasts. And she couldn't control the expressive way that her shoulder lifted, her throat arching to the erotic suck of his mouth.

'Mmm,' he murmured, drawing her backward against his warm body. 'You taste of clean water and that delicious flavour called Annie. I am addicted,' he confessed. 'I shall now require the taste of her several times a day.'

She quivered at his provocatively teasing banter, but had no equally provocative answer ready to offer him. This kind of situation was so new to her that she was quite frankly at a loss as to what to do or say.

Then his hands shifted upwards, and she arched convulsively on a sharp, indrawn rasp of air. 'Don't touch!' she gasped.

He went still for a moment, then turned her to face him, water gushing over her shoulders to splash onto the whorls of dark hair on his chest as he searched her anxious eyes, then her blushing cheeks, then finally the way her bent arms braced against his chest in an effort to keep his body away from her wet, silky breasts. 'Ah,' he said, then surprised her with the smuggest, most sensually triumphant grin that she had ever seen.

'It isn't funny!' she flashed out indignantly. 'They hurt!'

'Poor Annie,' he murmured in sympathy, but his grin widened, the man in him annoyingly proud that his loving could have such a lingering effect.

Then he swooped, taking one engorged nipple into his mouth and sucking so ruthlessly that she cried out, then gasped, then quivered as pain became a piercing pleasure.

If she'd worried about how she was going to face him this morning then that worry became swallowed up by what happened next.

It was as erotic as it was unconventional to her untutored soul. What with the warm water gushing, ignored, over both of them and his hands sliding down her supple spine to gather her against the rhythmic probing thrust of his hips, he ignited her desire for him so quickly that the night before might not have taken place.

His mouth lifted to capture her own, and, hungry, searching, they strained against each other while his loose hair received the full flood of warm water, plastering the satin pelt to both their faces, water running in rivulets down their noses and circling their joined mouths.

He broke the contact to drag in a harsh breath, his big chest lifting and falling in a tortured rasp. Then he was taking hold of her arms and urging them around his neck before he clasped her just below her buttocks, forcing her legs apart and around his tight waist as he lifted her up against him. His smooth, slick entry literally took her breath away.

Then the shower snapped off, and this latest variation on the act of love was achieved in a cubicle engulfed in warm, sensual steam...

For days they carried on like that—long, lazy, sensual days when they seemed to become so absorbed in each other that they could put the rest of the world right away.

The ate together, they slept together, they played in the sea or simply lazed beneath the shade of one of the big flame-trees together, supposedly content to read a novel each, but really it was usually just another way of enjoying the sexual tension always, always present between them. Her fingers trailed delicately over the fine, crisp hairs on his arm as she read; his hands lightly caressed her sun-kissed thigh as he did the same.

And, of course, they made love all the time—any time. His appetite seemed utterly insatiable, and hers rose greedily to meet his with little encouragement.

But that didn't mean she didn't have moments when she allowed her thoughts to drift towards the blunt reality of why they were here at all. But if she so much as mentioned home or work or, more importantly, the obligation they both had to Todd and *Cliché*, he would simply shut her up in the most effective way he could find.

Sex. But she did allow herself to wonder, during those few brief moments before he made her lose touch with the sensible part of her mind, if these were deliberate manoeuvres applied to stall her for some deep, dark reason of his own.

The trouble was that she *wanted* to be manoeuvred. She *wanted* to think of nothing else but this and him and—God—make believe it all really meant something.

Why? she asked herself frowningly one morning when she sat modestly covered by her bathrobe in front of her mirror, rubbing at her damp hair with a towel.

And she was almost bowled over by the power of the answer which suddenly erupted inside her. Her hand went still, she looked up and focused on the new, helplessly vulnerable expression now colouring her blue eyes.

No. She shook her head, glanced away, refused to accept it. She could not be falling in love with him as well!

As well as what? she asked herself tautly.

As well as being so sexually obsessed by him that she could barely look at him without wanting him badly!

'Damn,' she muttered shakily, glad that he was still in the bathroom and therefore not there to witness this revealing bit of self-analysis taking place.

Love. She tried tasting the word carefully.

Had she become one of those poor, wretched creatures—a woman in love?

God. Yes, she admitted, and covered those knowing eyes with a decidedly shaky hand.

She was in love with him. Of course she was in love with him, or why else had she let herself become such a slave to all of this?

And it isn't even real! She pulled her head away from her hand to take that blunt realisation full in the face. This—all of this had begun as one huge set-up!

A week ago he was committed to hurting you, Annie! she told herself. And, despite what happened in between, a few days ago he was still using blackmail to force you to bend to his will!

And what about Todd? Did he still intend using his power as Adamas to make Todd bend to his will?

She knew by experience that he could be downright ruthless with that power. Susie meant a lot to him—he had said as much during their fight down on the beach the other day.

But—now? After all of—this? Was he still intent on forcing a split between herself and Todd simply for his cousin's sake?

César used that moment to walk into the room, arrogant in his nakedness. Annie—in breathless silence, via the mirror—watched him saunter towards her, bend to brace himself with his hands against the dressing table, either side of her body, smile a heart-achingly tender smile into her wary eyes then lower his head to taste her throat, his damp hair swinging in a slick, heavy pelt to one side.

Could this man who could smile at her like that still want to put his cousin's feelings before her own?

'César...' she murmured hesitantly, her blue eyes anxious as they watched him nuzzle her throat.

'Hmm?' She quivered as the soft sound vibrated across her skin. He felt the response and did it again. Only the 'hmm' this time was an expression of pleasure.

Annie closed her eyes and tried very hard to concentrate—not on him but on the question she wanted to ask.

'Todd,' she said. 'What are you going to do about Todd and the *Cliché* launch?'

He went still for a moment, his mouth warm where it rested against her softly throbbing pulse. Then, 'This is no longer your problem,' he dismissed, returning his attention to her throat.

'But of course it's my problem!' she insisted, trying to arch away from his seeking lips. 'I'm worried about the *Cliché* launch!'

'Worry about me instead,' he said huskily, and sucked the small fleshy lobe of her ear into his mouth.

She quivered, lips parting on a soft gasp of stinging pleasure. 'Stop it!' she said, determinedly pulling away. 'We need to talk.'

There was another moment's silence when she thought he was going to ignore her—once again. His head remained bent, his hands braced either side of her. Then he straightened, and his eyes when they connected with hers via the mirror were suddenly inscrutable.

'So, talk,' he conceded coolly.

Her heart gave a small flutter—cowardice, she recognised, wanting to drop the whole subject before she spoiled what they had going here. But...

'What are you going to do about me?' she said. 'And Todd and his magazine launch?'

'You forgot to add Susie into that equation,' he inserted, turning away.

'Susie?' Twisting around on the stool, she stared up at him. 'But I don't understand.' She frowned. 'Everything's changed now! Surely you aren't still intending to—?'

'And what has changed exactly?' he drawled as he moved with a lithe, arrogant grace back across the bedroom.

Her heart took up a slow, heavy pumping as she watched him go, the rear view almost as excruciatingly desirable as the front view. The man had muscles where muscles ought not to be!

'Y-you know I'm no threat to Susie's personal relationship with Todd,' she reminded him huskily, having to struggle to subdue the feelings that were threatening to divert her from the subject in hand. 'But our business relationship is different! I won that contract fair and square, César. And neither you nor Susie can have any justification in wanting to take it away from me now!'

'You still want to keep it?' Reaching around the open bathroom door, he hooked a clean towel from the rail inside while holding her gaze with a cool, questioning look.

She frowned. 'Of course I want to keep it.'

'Why?'

'Why should I not want to?' she countered.

'Maybe because I am asking you not to,' he suggested quietly, wrapping the towel around his lean hips.

Annie came stiffly to her feet, not sure whether the sudden movement was brought on by the discomfiting subject matter of this conversation or because of the blatant sensuality with which this man did everything— even held this damned conversation!

'And why should *you* want to do that?' she demanded.

'Because this particular contract is just one job among many jobs to you,' he replied, with a dismissive shrug of one taut, bronzed shoulder. 'But to Susie it would be the making of her career. Oh,' he continued when Annie opened her mouth to speak, 'I know she's good. But she's not in your league, Angelica. You can survive without the big boost the *Cliché* launch will give your career, whereas Susie's career will probably never really recover from losing that contract to you in the first place.'

Her eyes widened at this cool business assessment he made of both herself and Susie. 'So you want me to give it all up for Susie's sake?' she choked in blank disbelief.

'Would that be such a very big hardship to you?'

Was that a question or a not very subtle statement of command? she wondered. Then sat down again slowly—very slowly because it suddenly occurred to her that it didn't matter whether it was a question or not. The very fact that he was making the sounds at all was enough to make her legs tremble so badly that she had a fear that they would collapse if she did not keep them under strict control.

Betrayed, she realised painfully. She was feeling betrayed on every level. Betrayed by the subterfuge he had used to get her here to this island in the first place. Betrayed by his later remorse and apparent desire to put things right once he'd realised his mistake, and betrayed by the depth of intimacy he had used to bring her oh, so cunningly to this moment of truth.

And all of it—all of it done in Susie Frazer's name. Blow his own sister! Blow Luis Alvarez! This—everything that had taken place over the last week—had simply been manoeuvre and counter-manoeuvre on his part, with this one goal in mind!

To make Annie Lacey malleable enough to do anything for him that he asked of her.

What a bloody fool she had been. Now she felt sick.

'What are you thinking?' His voice seemed to reach her from down a long, dark tunnel.

'I'm thinking you're a bastard,' she whispered thickly.

Silence.

Her eyelashes flickered, then lifted to allow her eyes to focus on him. He was standing there across the room like some—some noble Apache chief! she likened wretchedly. Wearing that skimpy white towel like a loin-cloth that left too much naked, bronzed muscle on show! His hair was hanging sleek and straight to the proud set of his shoulders while those crazy green eyes of his looked down that long, arrogant nose at her as if he couldn't believe that this *woman* could dare to insult him like that!

Then he sighed and moved in a grim gesture of impatience. 'Dammit, but you are my wife now, Angelica!' he exclaimed, with what she saw as an appalling confirmation of his arrogance. 'You do not need to do that kind of work any more! Whereas Susie—'

'Wife?' From somewhere—she didn't know where—anger took over from nausea and shot her furiously back to her feet. 'And when exactly did I become your wife, César?' she demanded with a withering scorn. 'From the moment you realised that your and Susie's plans were no longer justified, so you had to find another way to keep me here incarcerated on this island?'

'Don't be stupid!' he snapped, beginning to stride towards her. 'I told you I had no intention of harming you! Why can't you show me a little trust?'

Trust. There was that rotten word again.

'What is there to trust?' she demanded bitterly. 'Your word—when you've done nothing but break it since I met you?'

'Just because I asked for a little common charity does not mean I am about to break my word to you!' he rasped as he reached her.

'No? Well, my answer is a clear-cut, unequivocal no. I won't hand over the *Cliché* job to Susie.' Her blue eyes lifted to challenge him with a look of fierce contempt. 'So where do we go form here? César—hmm?' she taunted dangerously. 'Where...?'

CHAPTER TEN

To HELL, apparently. They went to hell, Annie decided later as she lay in the middle of the rumpled bed that César had just stalked angrily away from—after taking her to hell by the most exciting route he could find.

And now she lay devastated, maybe suffering from shock—she wasn't sure. All she did know was that that one small question had exploded into a blistering row and from the blistering row had come the blistering sex.

But, worse, she had not been dragged down into the fiery depths of that hell protesting. No, she'd gone willingly—eagerly!

'Oh, God,' she groaned, rolling onto her side so that she could bury her shame in the snowy white pillow.

His pillow. A pillow that held the scent of him. And almost instantly she was assailed with the kind of thoughts and feelings that cruelly mocked the sense of shame.

It wasn't as if she could even comfort herself with the knowledge that she'd tried to fight him off! Because she hadn't.

From the moment his hands had reached out to take hold of her she had lost all sense of reason. Pure sexual exhilaration had fizzed up from the centre of her fury to coil in a hot, pulsing constriction around the muscles of her womanhood, and she'd gone, kicking, scratching, biting, into the fiery vats of passion with him, giving him back kiss for savage kiss, caress for ravaging caress until the whole wild battle had finally converged in a soul-destroying climax which had left her dead-limbed, mind-blown and spent, and him punching the pillow with a white-knuckled fist as he fought to regain control of his shattered emotions.

Then, 'Damn you,' he'd muttered to her as he'd climbed off the bed. 'Damn you to bloody hell for making me behave like that!'

If he'd called her Annie the super-tramp he could not have hurt her more than that angry damning did.

Then she heard it, and her head picked up, ears tensed and listening to the faint, deep whooshing sound that took a few moments to register in her sluggish brain.

No, she thought hectically. She refused to believe it— not after what had just taken place on this bed! No!

Suddenly she was jackknifing to her feet, fingers scrambling, body trembling in her haste as she dragged the rumpled sheet with her and began draping the fine cloth around her body even as she ran out of the open French windows and onto the upper balcony.

The sun was high, blinding as it hit her eyes, and she almost lost the sheet altogether when she instinctively lifted a hand to shade out the brightness. Then she saw it, hovering just twenty feet from the ground, the powerful whir of blades shattering the still air with its blunt, cruel statement.

'No, César,' she whispered, tripping over the trailing sheet as she staggered to the balcony rail. 'Don't you dare. Don't you dare!'

But he did dare, apparently. And it felt as if everything living inside her took a swooping dive to her stomach as the helicopter slowly turned until it was facing out to sea, then shot forward, leaving her leaning there against the balcony rail, watching it go, while hot tears of bitter helplessness ran unchecked down her cheeks.

It hurt. His cruel desertion of her hurt. The fact that he could leave her here like this after what had just taken place in the bedroom behind her—hurt.

Where was he going? Why was he going? Was he going to find Susie to explain that he couldn't make Annie Lacey bend totally to his will?

A whole week she was left alone to stew in her own bitterness, seven long frustrating days and nights when all she did was consolidate every bad thought that she had ever had about him. It was a week in which she barely left the villa and had Margarita fussing around her like a worried hen as her moods swung from anger to hurt and from hurt to wretched tears and from tears to a cold, dark depression that refused to lift no matter how often she told herself that none of it was worth this much grief.

On the eighth day she was sitting in the coral-coloured sitting room when the familiar sounds of helicopter blades heralded his return.

Her heart skipped a couple of beats, but other than that she didn't move, did not lift her eyes from the paperback that she was supposed to be reading. For the space of thirty long, taut seconds she showed no visible sign at all that his return interested her in the slightest...

Then smoothly, coolly, calmly she got up, walked out of the room and up the stairs to her bedroom.

She was methodically folding clothes into her suitcase when he appeared in the doorway. She felt his arrival, felt his sudden stillness when he saw what she was doing, felt his eyes home sharply in on her—and didn't even grace him with a glance.

'What are you doing?' he demanded finally.

She didn't bother to answer the obvious either, her hands remaining steady as they settled soft, silky underwear in the suitcase lying open on the stand by the bathroom door.

'I'll be ready to leave in a few minutes,' she informed him instead.

Silence. A silence so taut that it made her ears begin to tingle and her chest grow tight. Then, 'Don't be foolish!' he said roughly, striding further into the room to throw something onto the nearby tabletop. 'You are not going anywhere. OK, so you are angry with me,' he allowed magnanimously. 'I acknowledge it.'

Big of you, she thought, and continued back to the dressing table to begin emptying the next drawer.

His eyes followed her in pulsing frustration. 'Angelica...' he sighed, reaching out with a hand to stop her as she went to walk past him.

She turned on him like a rattlesnake. Then wished to God that she hadn't when she felt herself hit by the full, stinging blast of his grim, dark attraction.

Why do you do this to me? she screamed out in silent anguish as her senses caught alight and began crackling like a flash-fire through her blood.

He was standing there in the immaculate clothes of a businessman. Plain grey tie worn over a crisp white shirt. Plain grey twill trousers sitting perfectly on the top of polished black shoes. The epitome of convention in fact. While that hair of his, so arrogantly contained in is slender black ribbon, shrieked 'Rogue' at her! 'Scoundrel! For God's sake watch out!'

'Don't you touch me!' she spat at him in sheer re-action. 'Don't you—' disgustedly she wiped his hand from her arm '—dare touch me!'

His chin went up, his eyes alight with the green, green glow of affronted pride, his chiselled mouth pulling into a straight, flat line that did nothing—nothing to spoil its innate sex appeal! While she just stood here, breasts heaving, eyes defying him, waiting with her senses on full alert to see how he was going to react to that little bit of ego-squashing.

'Look...' he muttered after another tense pause. 'This is crazy.'

Her word, Annie thought possessively. Crazy. Her whole existence had been crazy from the moment she'd first set eyes on him!

'What do you want me to say, Angelica? That I am sorry? That I should not have left here the way that I did? I know it,' he accepted. 'You know it! But I had to leave. I did not like what we were doing to each other. I needed to be alone—to think—to try to find a—'

'Well, at least you had the *choice* whether to go or stay!'

There was another short silence while he took on board the full import of that last remark. Then he gave another heavy sigh, and the muscles in her chest began to throb. She wasn't sure why. They just did, holding her tense and still and so utterly miserable that she wanted to weep.

'I just want to leave here,' she repeated thickly. 'Now— as soon as it can be arranged.'

'We have to talk.'

She shook her head. 'What is there left to talk about?' she asked. 'The *Cliché* launch?' Her mouth took on a bitter twist that mocked the whole subject. 'I'm no longer interested in discussing that with you,' she announced. 'Not any of it.'

'And why not?' he asked grimly. 'It meant all the world to you a week ago.'

'A week ago I was still living in cloud-cuckoo-land,' she derided. 'Since then, and while you've been off having your lonely think, I've been having mine. And I want out. Out of this house and this island, out of any commitment I may have to you so I can go and deal with my own commitments myself.'

Take that, you arrogant devil, she thought, and turned stiffly away.

'You said you'd wait until we knew if there was a child or not.'

She paused half a stride back to her suitcase, her eyes closing on a moment's frozen stillness. When they opened again the blue was empty—as empty as she was feeling inside right now.

'There isn't going to be a child,' she told him huskily, and continued jerkily on her way. 'So that's it,' she went on in a tone that said she didn't care, when really she had cared. It had come as yet another devastating blow to find out how much she had cared about carrying his baby. 'All promises to you fulfilled,' she stated. 'Now I want you to fulfil your promise to me and let me go.'

'You could be lying...' he drawled, his eyes narrowing in suspicion at her carefully controlled voice.

'You expected me to preserve the evidence?' she mocked with crude sarcasm.

He didn't like to hear it from her. The sudden black flash of disapproval in his eyes told her that he didn't like it. 'Don't talk like that,' he said grimly. 'It degrades you.'

She swung round. 'And you think it isn't degrading to have my word questioned as you just did?' she threw back.

His mouth closed tight, his face with it. 'So you want to leave,' he said quietly after a moment.

She nodded. Mute. Determined.

He let out a short sigh. 'We have something good going for us here, Angelica, if you could try to show me a little trust.'

Trust. There was that word again—trust.

'And what is there to trust exactly?' she derided. 'When none of this has been real?'

'It's been real enough!' he countered. 'This is real!' Stepping forward, he reached out to grab hold of her hand and tugged it out in front of them both so that the band of gold on her finger glinted in the sunlight. 'We made solemn vows to each other and signed a legal document to make it real!'

'I'm not talking legally, I'm talking personally!' Angrily she snatched back the hand, clenching her fingers over the ring that was to her only a sham, like the vows they shared and the document they'd signed. 'You—me—actually meaning those vows we said to each other! That wasn't real!' Her tight mouth quivered. 'Yet we both had the gall to behave as if they were.'

'We like making love to each other,' he pointed out.

She sighed, but didn't deny it. He was right, after all—they did like making love. Revelled in each other, in fact. Drowned in each other.

'We like being with each other. We like talking together and laughing together—or even fighting together as we are doing now!'

'I'm not the one fighting here!' she denied vehemently. 'All I'm trying to do is get packed to go home! I hate all this fighting we do,' she added as a muttered aside.

To her utter annoyance he laughed! 'Liar,' he said. 'You love it. It excites you. Just the same as it excites me to fight with you.'

'Is that supposed to be some kind of joke?' she gasped in choking indignation.

'I am not joking,' he denied. 'I tell you—' His hands slapped a brazen gesture on the top of his thighs. 'No joke,' he claimed, drawing her angry eyes downwards.

And dark heat rumbled into her face when she saw what was happening to him. 'You're disgusting,' she snapped, looking angrily away.

'I am a man,' he replied, as if that made everything acceptable.

'And an arrogant one.'

'I do not deny it.' He shrugged. 'But then,' he added silkily, 'I am not the one denying anything here.'

'Why don't you go to hell?' she flashed, for want of a better answer to that.

'What—again?'

Her insides jumped, blue eyes flickering warily upwards to catch the way that those sleek black brows of his had arched in a gesture of mocking knowledge. So he too had seen that last sexual battle they'd fought as a visit to hell, she realised with a sudden flutter of alarm as he began to walk towards her.

'How nice of you to offer,' he went on silkily. 'Thank you, I think I will...'

And she began backing. 'Don't you come near me!' she choked, her heart pumping dangerously fast, hands held out in front of her as if to ward off the devil.

He reached the hands; they flattened against his rock-solid chest. Eyes narrowed and glinting bright green with intention, he herded her backwards like a piece of cattle until her back made thudding contact with the wall. And still he kept on coming, until her braced arms buckled beneath the strain and his body was making full and dangerous contact with her own. In all her life she had never felt so intimidated—or so exhilarated!

'No!' she gasped out breathlessly. 'Please, César! Don't!'

Too late, his dark head was already lowering, his mouth hot as it made contact with hers. She could feel his heart pumping beneath her spread palms, could feel the warmth of his body, the powerful muscles, felt his tongue run in a moist, sensual slide across her tightly clamped lips.

And in seconds she could feel herself surrendering, her mouth wanting to part, her tongue to join with his, her fingers trembling with a desperate need to rip open his shirt and bury themselves in the crisp, dark hair covering his chest—the whole lot threatening to fling her screaming with delight into that wild, hot well of passion.

Oh, God, she thought dizzily. But she wished that she could hate him! She knew that she *should* hate him! She *wanted* to hate him! But she didn't. She loved him!

With a sob of anguish she tried to thrust him away. He growled something impatient, brought his hands snaking up to rake roughly through her hair—cupping her head—arching it backwards—long thumbs sliding across her heated cheeks to hold her face up to his— enthralling her with the urgency with which he forced her lips apart and hungrily deepened the kiss.

And in an act of sheer self-preservation she gave a violent push at his shoulders and managed to wrench her throbbing mouth to one side. It stopped him. His dark head came up, his big chest heaving, his own cheeks flushed with desire, and his eyes barely focused as they stared at her.

'If you've quite finished,' she heard herself say with unbelievable cool, 'then I would now like to get packed and leave.'

He was suddenly very still, the new silence beating like a hundred war drums inside her head as she stood there defying him with her eyes. Ever since she'd met him—all along the line!—she'd given in to him. But this time—this time she was determined to win.

And at last and finally he must have realised it, be- cause his eyes went black with anger then cold as pale green ice. He took a step back from her, severing all body contact like a scalpel slicing through flesh.

'OK, Angelica,' he said grimly. 'If that is what you want. You win.'

With that he turned and walked out of the room.

'You win', she repeated dully to herself as she wilted against the wall behind her, eyes closing, heart hurting at the prize that she had just managed to win for herself.

Freedom, she supposed you'd call it. She'd just won the freedom to choose to leave here at last.

So why did she feel as if she'd just lost the biggest prize of her life?

No, that's weak thinking, Annie, she told herself grimly. He doesn't love you. He wants you, she conceded bitterly. He desires your body like crazy, and he's possessive and territorial about it. But that isn't love.

A man in love doesn't lie and cheat and connive to trap. He doesn't blackmail and bully and seduce and— Oh, shut up! she told her hectic brain. Shut up! Stop rubbing it in!

Eyes flying open with a flash of pained anger, she thrust herself away from the wall—

It was then that she saw it—a brown paper package lying askew on the pale wood tabletop. Her mind did a flashback of César tossing it there.

Slowly, uncertainly she began to walk towards it. Drawn there. Unable to resist.

It was an envelope, she realised. A special kind of envelope. Big, rectangular, card-backed. Her mouth went dry, clammy sweat breaking out all over her as she recognised it instantly for what it had to be.

The kind of envelope a photographer put prints in.

Her flesh began to tingle with a new guilt-ridden fear, and she knew why. She was going to look inside it— knew she couldn't stop herself. Even though she knew with a cold sense of anguish just what she was going to see.

Susie decked out for the *Cliché* launch.

It had to be. What else could it be?

Fingers trembling, heart hammering, she slipped open the flap and slowly slid the contents onto the shiny tabletop.

For a dozen heart-stunning moments she was completely unmoving. Didn't breathe, didn't blink, didn't function at all on any human level.

Because they were not photographs of Susie.

Tears blurred her eyes, hot and burning, catching as a sob in her throat.

They were not even photographs in the true sense.

They were mock-ups of the front and centre-fold pages of a magazine—'CLICHÉ' superimposed in red across a beautiful Caribbean blue sky.

'Oh, God,' she whispered as she stared at them, a hand jerking up to cover her trembling mouth.

There was an old saying about cameras never lying. But, being a professional model, Annie knew this to be an utter untruth. Cameras could and did lie—all the time.

But this camera wasn't lying. The camera that took these pictures was so glaringly obviously telling the truth that no one—no one who looked at these images in front of her could even begin to doubt that what was being shown was the truth.

Two people about to marry each other.

Two people decked out in white and gazing into each other's eyes with such a bitter-sweet intensity that it was as clear and clean and spiritual as the smile on the minister's face in the background that these two people were madly, blindly in love.

'But I didn't even know then,' she whispered to herself in thickened dismay.

'I did.'

With a shaken gasp she spun around to find César leaning in the open doorway to the balcony.

Dark colour flooded into her cheeks then drained away again, leaving her pale and shocked by what he had just said.

'Why didn't you tell me about these?' she asked shakily.

He had his hands stuck in the pockets of his grey trousers. She couldn't see his face because the sun was right behind him, but she saw a broad shoulder lift and fall in a lazy shrug. 'There never seemed to be an—appropriate moment,' he replied very drily, referring, she presumed, to the fact that they'd started fighting almost from the moment he'd come into the room. 'Do you still want to leave here?' he asked suddenly.

She shook her head, tears blurring out her vision.

'Good,' he replied, but his tone was oddly flat and reserved. It held her back from running to him as she wanted to do. And there was a decided reticence about the slow way he straightened himself then came further into the room.

'Those pictures are the reason I was away so long,' he explained. 'I had to go to London. To see your half-brother. We—talked,' he said, after a small pause which suggested that they'd done a whole lot more than just talk. 'About you, mainly. But also about the *Cliché* launch.' Another pause, and again she received the odd impression that he was telling her all of this with constraint.

Was he still angry because she'd rejected him a few minutes ago? she wondered. Was he waiting for her to apologise, beg forgiveness?

'Hanson had those mock-ups done for his first issue, but if you don't want it splattered all over the world then we won't do it.' Another shrug and he had reached the end of the bed. 'But...'

Ah, Annie thought, and stiffened, the cynical side to her nature recognising that there was usually a big 'but' to most things.

'I had trouble convincing him of a few—provisos of my own before I would give permission.'

'What provisos?' she asked warily. She didn't like this—she didn't like any of it. She had just experienced the absolute beauty of discovering that the man she was in love with loved her too, yet the whole thing was being so thoroughly dampened by his manner that she was already beginning to doubt what her own eyes had told her those photographs claimed!

'There are two envelopes on the table, Angelica,' he pointed out.

'Two?' She glanced back at the table, then made a sound of surprise. He was right, and there were two! She hadn't noticed.

'It has to be sheer fluke that you opened the right one first,' he then said drily. 'Or I don't think you would be standing there eating me with your beautiful eyes as you have been doing.'

Sarcasm, dry and taunting. It hurt.

'Open it,' he commanded.

She shook her head. She didn't want to. There was going to be something horrible in that other envelope, or why else would he have said what he'd just said?

'This is it, Angelica,' he stated quietly. 'The point where you learn you were right not to trust me. Open it,' he repeated. 'Open it.'

Reluctantly she pulled the other envelope towards her. Lips dry, fingers shaking, she opened the flap then slid the contents out.

No mock-ups this time, she noted on a sickly hot wave of disenchantment, but glossy seven-by-nines. Professional photographs—of Susie. Susie in white, wearing rubies. Susie in gold, wearing emeralds. Susie in black, wearing the most beautiful diamonds... Tears flashed across her eyes as slowly, shakily, with the silence growing thick all around her, she looked at each photograph in turn—a half-dozen of them in all.

'No sapphires,' she murmured finally.

'No,' he confirmed. 'No sapphires.'

Hurt blue eyes flicked around to search out his. 'Why not?'

There wasn't a hint of emotion showing in those steady green eyes. 'They're yours,' he reminded her quietly.

That was all he said, and, swallowing thickly, she looked away from him again. 'Did you ever intend using me for this shoot?'

'No.' Just as quiet, just as lacking in emotion. She flinched.

'You see, I promised Susie years ago that the next time I put a collection together she could show it,' he explained in that same quiet, flat voice. 'It isn't her fault that I decided to use the Adamas name as bait to hook you, Angelica. That was my decision. Those pictures were taken weeks ago—well before Hanson made his decision to use you instead of Susie for his launch. I made that promise to her in good faith and I couldn't, in all fairness, break it simply because I had made the damned thing so complicated.'

Which was why he had tried so hard to talk her round that day before he'd left, Angelica realised. And at last began to understand the full tangle that this web of conspiracy had got into.

'She loves Hanson, dammit!' he suddenly exploded when she showed no sign that any of what he'd said had got through to her. 'And she believed that he loved her! On the strength of that love she'd constructed this great plan where he chose her to launch *Cliché* and she came up with the biggest scoop for his first issue he could possibly hope for! I'd even gone to London specially to be there when she did it!' A sigh rasped harshly from him. 'Have you any idea how deeply he hurt her when he chose you instead of her?'

'Yes,' she whispered, because she was feeling a little of how that hurt felt herself right now. 'Has Todd seen these?' she then asked quietly.

'Yes,' he sighed. 'He's seen them. I took them with me to try to make him see some sense about Susie. He didn't,' he clipped. 'The man is—'

Hurt, Annie put in silently when César cut the rest of the sentence off. Not that 'hurt' was what César had been going to say, she noted from the angry look on his face.

'Anyway,' he went on, 'I've offered him a deal whereby he can launch *Cliché* with our wedding—hence the mock-ups—' he indicated them with his hand. 'So long as he fronts Susie and the Adamas collection in his second issue.'

She said nothing, her blonde head bowed over the two different sets of photographs scattered on the table.

'I'm sorry if you feel I have forfeited your feelings with this decision,' he went on heavily after a moment. 'But, being faced with the dilemma I had made for myself, I saw no other way out without hurting someone, and ...'

My feelings were easier to hurt than Susie's, she silently finished for him when he stopped, shrugging eloquently instead.

'And Todd agreed?' she asked.

'No,' he said. 'He is considering my offer as we speak and is due here in a couple of days with his decision.' Another sigh, and the atmosphere in the sunny room thickened a little more. 'He already had a fair idea of what has been going on here, Angelica,' he informed her. 'We were caught by a Press photographer in that tight embrace when I poured the champagne over you the first night we met. The picture appeared in the paper the next morning.'

More bad publicity, she thought, and shuddered.

'Hanson recognised me as the same man who had let him discover the Adamas identity that same night,' he went on. 'Almost immediately my real name DeSanquez struck a chord in his brain, connecting me with the Alvarez affair, and since then he has been tearing his hair out trying to trace where you'd been taken. He was worried about you,' he huskily confessed. 'Frightened because he had to suspect me of planning the whole thing for the purposes of revenge and...' His expressive shrug acknowledged how accurately Todd had put the full picture together. 'So I had to do some quick thinking if I was going to stop him from guessing the rest.'

'And said—what?' she asked, turning coolly to face him.

He was half leaning, half sitting on the edge of the dressing table, outwardly perfectly relaxed—if you didn't notice the tell-tale nerve working in his jaw.

But his eyes were studiedly impassive as he continued. 'I told him the truth,' he answered simply, then almost immediately qualified that remark. 'Or the truth as far as it was necessary, anyway.' And the smile that played briefly around his mouth hinted at just which part he had left out. The big love scene—their big love scene. The one that had ripped a gaping hole in the Annie Lacey persona. 'Then I showed him the pictures of our wedding day and let them speak for me.'

'And did they?'

'Oh, yes.' He smiled. 'They speak loud and clear to anyone who looks at them, don't you think?'

She refused to take him up on that one; there was still too much left to be said. 'And Susie?' she prompted. 'What did you tell him about Susie's involvement in it all?'

'I told him that Susie knew nothing of what I had planned for you here,' he stated flatly.

But her sceptical look made him sigh with impatience.

'It's the truth,' he insisted. 'Susie knew nothing! Which is why it is so unfair for her to pay the price for my sins. She loves Hanson!' he declared. 'And whatever slant you want to put on it your relationship with him did look suspect! She had a right to feel jealous, used, unfairly treated!

'And, yes,' he added before Angelica could say it herself, 'she hated you for being what she saw as the woman who was wrecking her life on both personal and professional counts. But her hatred stopped short of plotting with me against you. I didn't need her help to plot,' he then said drily. 'I am cunning enough to manage without the need of an accomplice.'

'You threw that champagne over me deliberately,' she pointed out.

His wry half-nod acknowledged it.

'It was Susie who took great delight in telling Todd all about the embrace which followed,' she added. 'She knew exactly who you were.'

'And that part, I concede, was a set-up. But only in as far as I promised to get you out of the way so she could talk to Hanson. As to the rest—she was then and still is totally in the dark!'

Did she believe him? Annie shifted restlessly. She wanted to believe him. It was easier on her pride to believe that Susie knew nothing of what had been planned on this island for her arch-rival Annie Lacey.

'So, why are you telling me all of this?' she asked carefully.

'Because,' he said quietly, 'I need your support when Hanson gets here. I need you to help convince him that Susie is the innocent party in all of this, and that you really don't mind that Susie has taken the Adamas scoop from you.

'It's important to her, Angelica,' he added roughly, when her cool face gave him no hint at all as to what she was thinking. 'It is important to Hanson that he is offered a way to—give a little where she is concerned! He is in love with Susie, but, as you once told me yourself, he is capable of never forgiving her if he truly believes she collaborated with me against you.

'Please,' he appealed, 'in the face of what those mock-ups tell us, show a little compassion for someone less fortunate in love than yourself and back me up in all of this.'

She moved at long last, shifting out of her cool, still stance to turn back to the array of photo work littered across the table. Her fingers flittered across those of Susie and settled on one of César and herself. It was one in which the photographer had captured the moment when César had slid the rings onto her finger. His dark head was bent, his lean profile taut, his mouth straight and flat and grim. But the eyes were alive—looking at her while she looked at the rings—alive with a burning, helpless—

'No...' she whispered, beginning to gather up with trembling fingers every mock-up lying there. 'I d-don't care what you do with the Adamas thing. Susie can keep it. It doesn't matter a jot to me. But—' she turned, clutching the mock-ups possessively to her chest '—I won't allow you to publish these, César. I won't,' she warned him defiantly. 'I won't let you make a public spectacle out of these!'

CHAPTER ELEVEN

' "A SPECTACLE"?' César's lean body came out of its casual resting position to shoot stiffly to its full, impressive height in affront. 'What do you mean, "a spectacle"?' he demanded. Then he added icily, 'Are you saying that you look on our marriage as a joke?'

'No!' she sighed, wondering how a man with all his arrogance could be so damned touchy sometimes! 'But look at these, César!' she pleaded, her hand coming out shakily to offer the mock-ups. 'Look how beautiful they are. How—special!' she cried. 'Too special to have them made a public mockery of!'

'A mockery?' His frown was dark, his face an angry map of puzzled indignity as he looked from her anxious face to the mock-ups then back again. 'I don't understand. Why should anyone want to mock them?'

'Because out there I am still Annie Lacey the notorious man-eater!' She spelled it out rawly. 'And they'll be shocked that you of all people would marry me!'

'Who?' he demanded. 'Who, in your estimation, is that crass-minded?'

Her eyes closed briefly on a tense, tight sigh. 'The Press,' she said. 'They can be so vicious when they get their teeth into someone—you know that! They'll slay you the moment they see these photographs!' Her chest heaved on a wretched indrawn breath.

'Then they'll dredge it all up again, replay the whole Luis Alvarez nightmare again. They'll mock Todd for printing the wedding pictures of his long-term on-and-off lover—and you for being stupid enough to take me

176

on! Th-then they'll mention your sister,' she concluded thickly, 'and wonder how you could marry the woman who wrecked your own sister's marriage!'

'So you would prefer to hide our marriage away like some dark secret rather than face the world with what those pictures show as the truth?' Sighing tightly, he came to take the mock-ups from her and tossed them contemptuously aside. 'Is this your novel way of telling me I have misread our whole relationship?' he said in a clipped voice.

'No!' She groaned at the interpretation that he had put on her words. 'Our marriage was a very special moment in my life! Those pictures make it special because they say so much to both of us!' Her eyes burned into him with a dark blue appeal. 'You're special to me,' she told him achingly. 'I'm thinking of you! I want to protect you! Not myself,' she dismissed. 'I couldn't care less about what they want to throw at me. But—'

He laughed! He was scornful, but he actually laughed. 'Do you mean,' he enunciated in choking disbelief, 'that you're making all this fuss—for my sake?' His hand snaked out, capturing hers so that he could tug her up against him. 'Look at me, Angelica,' he commanded grimly. 'Look into this face and tell me what you see.'

She looked, her eyes pained with love and bright with the unshed tears of her own uncertainties.

'Does this look like the face of a man who worries about what other people say or think about him?' he demanded. 'Does it?'

No, it did not. It looked like the face of a man hewn from the hardest, smoothest rock—a man as invincible as his Adamas trade-name implied him to be. The Spanish conquistador. The Apache chief. The face of arrogance personified.

The man she loved.

'But your sister isn't hewn from the same invulnerable mould as you, is she?' she pointed out wretchedly.

'Cristina?' He frowned, then bit out, 'To hell with Cristina. I've already spoken to her—told her the truth. She accepted it—painfully,' he acknowledged on a small, tight grimace that said that the truth had not been easy to take. 'But Cristina will be no problem to us. Unless,' he then added with a sudden sparkling wry humour, 'you allow for the way her guilty conscience will probably have her hounding you for the rest of her life—looking for her own redemption.'

'You're sure?' she murmured uncertainly.

'I am very sure,' he huskily confirmed.

Her soft mouth quivered. 'Then let go of my hand.'

'Why?' He frowned.

'I need something.'

Reluctantly he let go. Instantly she stepped closer, her fingers sliding over his muscled shoulder and around his strong neck, searching for, finding and curling around his tail of hair, then she buried her face in his warm throat and sighed as if she'd just been saved from drowning.

He muttered something and gathered her possessively in. 'What made you suddenly do that?' he asked tensely.

'Do what you like with the pictures,' she whispered into his taut throat. 'Give them to Todd—don't give them to Todd.' Her lips slid a sensual caress across his skin. 'I don't care,' she said. 'You're Adamas. Invincible. My rock. I'm marooning myself.'

'Ah,' he said, relaxing as he caught on. 'So you are relinquishing all responsibility to me?'

'That's right.' Her lips moved on to taste his chin. He needed a shave, so she stopped caressing and bit sensuously instead. 'You say you don't care what they throw at you, so—prove it. Publish and be damned,

Mr Adamas,' she challenged. 'Let them throw the lot at you—you can take it.

'I can just see the world headlines—SUPERMODEL ANNIE LACEY LANDS VENEZUELAN OIL BARON IN GRENADINE LOVE COUP!' she quoted. '"The price for exclusive rights to her body, a five-million-dollar sapphire and diamond-encrusted necklace from the Adamas collection, no less!"'

'Oh, please,' he drawled, the sound deep and sensually amused. 'GREAT GENIUS ADAMAS! I will not be upstaged by your supermodel status.'

She grinned, then stopped grinning to look seriously into his warmly laughing eyes. 'You're sure you don't mind?' she asked softly. 'That they're going to have a field-day with all of this?'

'Do I look as though I mind?' he murmured lazily.

'No,' she pouted. 'You look—'

She didn't manage to finish that sentence because the look was transformed into action—an action that had them tumbling onto the bed and into a wild, hot, passionate morass of sensual rediscovery.

'You were very rough on him,' Annie remarked a few days later as they stood together on the lower veranda, watching the helicopter that had brought Todd to the island that morning take him away again.

Todd had arrived in a belligerent mood, still unforgiving of Susie and determined to get the exclusive on Annie's marriage to César—without having Susie wearing the Adamas collection included in the deal.

He'd gone away conceding everything to a tough-talking, utterly immovable César—still belligerent, still feeling as if he had been manipulated by both César and Susie, but with his good business-sense winning over bruised ego in the end.

And the only consolation that he had gained from the whole episode was a total reassurance that Annie was exactly where she wanted to be.

'This whole business has been rough on everybody,' was César's unsympathetic reply to her now. 'I don't see why your half-brother should come out of it any less battle-scarred than the rest of us. Susie looked like a whipped dog that day he announced you were going to front his launch into Europe,' he added grimly. 'I don't know how I kept my hands off his cruel throat.'

'Poor Susie,' Annie sighed, turning to watch the helicopter fly out of sight. 'Do you think they'll manage to sort out their personal problems after this?' she asked worriedly.

'We have given them the means by which to keep communications open with the Adamas deal. The rest,' he said grimly, 'is up to them. But, you know, with a bit of trust on his side, Angelica, things need not have become as bad as they did for him and Susie.'

He was right, and she didn't argue with him. In fact, she had always tried to get Todd to tell Susie the truth about their own relationship, because she had known that it was causing unnecessary problems for both of them. If he had done, then maybe none of this would have happened.

Which was a bit of a double-edged sword, really, she mused wryly, because then she would not have been standing where she was standing right now—in the arms of the man she loved!

'And anyway,' César concluded with a shrug, 'I have no wish to dwell on their love-life any more than I have done already. My own love-life is complicated enough without taking on board their problems as well.'

'I am not complicated at all!' she denied, turning in the crook of his arm to glare at him. 'In fact—' she pouted '—I bet you've never had such an easy conquest as me! How long did it take?' she demanded. 'Twenty-four hours from meeting to getting me into your bed?'

He smiled with his mouth, but his eyes didn't; they darkened into a breathtaking seriousness. 'Four years,' he corrected. 'I spent four years aching for you. You tormented my mind, my heart, my empty soul...'

Sighing, he pulled her closer. 'I don't think I will ever come to terms with what one urgent phone call did to the next four years of my life,' he murmured heavily. 'I had it all set up—the party at my London apartment, the contact who would bring you to it. Then there was the teeth-gritting, electric anticipation of actually getting to meet you in the flesh at last. Then the call that forced me away that night.' His mouth tightened. 'And everything just seemed to fall apart around me. I hated Alvarez for doing that to me.'

'And hated me for letting him come near me,' she added hollowly.

'No!' He denied that. 'I hated you for ruining any hope I had of ever approaching you. Anyone else, Angelica,' he muttered painfully. 'Anyone else and it wouldn't have mattered. I am no prude! But my own sister's husband?' His sigh was tense. 'It left me with nothing—nothing to cling on to, you understand?'

'Don't,' she whispered, settling her trembling fingers against the grim tension of his mouth.

He kissed the fingers, but also dislodged them with a small, grim shake of his head. 'Then suddenly there you were again,' he continued, his eyes dark green with emotion. 'Being thrust into my life again, this time threatening Susie's happiness!'

'But—'

'Shush.' He silenced her. 'I will finish. Mistakes are mistakes, Angelica. All of us have had to acknowledge that one way or another over these last two weeks. But before the mistakes were exposed I had spent four years

seeing you as the kind of woman I could never care for—
should never care for,' he qualified.

Then he smiled very ruefully. 'It did not stop me from
wanting you, though,' he admitted, dropping a kiss on
her tender mouth. 'It simply turned that want into a
frustrated kind of ache that gnawed at me every time I
saw your face on a billboard or in a magazine or—' He
stopped and sighed.

'Then the Susie thing came up,' he went on. 'And, I
have to admit it, I was quite ready to pay you back for
four years of hell. I called it revenge for myself.'

He kissed her again before she could say anything.
'And I knew it the moment I saw you in the flesh that
night—it was the first time I had actually been in the
same company as you, did you know that?' His expression was wry. 'Four years lusting after one special
woman, and I hadn't even met her!'

'Fantasising gone mad.' She smiled.

He laughed, but it wasn't with any humour. 'A lot of
things gone mad,' he agreed. 'But I learned one very
dangerous thing on that first meeting. And it was that
holding you in my arms was like having all that madness
turning into sanity. It felt right,' he said softly. 'It felt
good! And, even more dangerous, I knew you too were
shocked by how good it felt.

'After that,' he claimed with more his usual arrogance, 'you really did not stand a chance. I may have
used all kinds of excuses for bringing you here, but I
knew deep down inside that I was bringing you here for
myself. I wanted you for myself. Susie no longer mattered. The Alvarez thing no longer mattered. From then
on the only mistakes being made were because of the
lies entangling both of us. I thought I was dealing with
a very spirited, very tough, very experienced woman.' If
it was possible, his eyes darkened even further. 'So I

made love to the woman I believed you to be, and found
I had defiled an angel—'

'No,' she protested. 'Don't call me that! It's not true
and I always hated it. It was just another lie I lived with,
can't you see that?' Her breasts moved against his chest
with a small heave of pain. 'Most of my life has been
spent playing a lie. First with my mother's help.' The
hurt that memory could still cause shot across her blue
eyes. 'Then as a silly character created to sell breakfast
cereal, for goodness' sake!'

'Don't cry,' he muttered when a film of tears washed
across her eyes.

'I'm not!' she denied, but the denial was thick with
tears too, and with a shaky sigh he captured her trembling mouth.

It was a now familiar kiss—the one that caught fire
at her lips and burned its way to every corner of her
body, cleansing all the bitterness and hurt right out of
her as it went. She sighed as she gave in to it, her soft
lips parting, her tongue searching, finding, and she gave
another pleasurable sigh as her hands went up around
his neck and found that shank of hair that she loved to
hold onto in moments like these.

It was wonderful—like coming home through the
storm and finding warmth and comfort waiting for her.
He pressed her against him and she melted into the embrace, loving the feel of her breasts cushioning against
the solid warmth of his chest, loving the feel of his body
alive and pulsing against her own.

He muttered something in Spanish as he drew away,
his eyes burning like angry green flames as they delved
into her own. 'You understand that I love you whoever
you are, whatever you are?'

'I understand,' she smiled softly.

He nodded, always arrogant, no matter what other
emotions were running rife through him. 'Angelica

DeSanquez,' he muttered, then added tersely, 'Remember how I said that! For Angelica Lacey no longer exists!'

'Did I tell you I'm madly in love with you?' she heard herself say, and actually cried out in alarm as he took her mouth again in a volcanic eruption of emotion that threatened to consume them both.

'You unman me,' he muttered hoarsely as his dark head dipped lower so that he could taste her silken throat. 'You always do. But then,' he added ruefully, 'I think you enjoy doing it.'

'You don't feel unmanned to me,' she remarked provocatively, nudging her hips against his swollen body.

His sigh was oddly shaken. 'Let go of my hair,' he ordered. 'You're hurting.'

'No.' Her grip only tightened as her mouth went in search of his ear to taste it. 'I like it,' she whispered. 'It's sexy.'

With a husky growl he bent and scooped her up into his arms.

'Where are we going?' she enquired innocently.

César sent her a glaring glance. 'Guess,' he mocked as he strode with grim intention into the coolness of the house.

Annie let go of the hair so she could trail a tender fingertip down his taut cheek. 'I love you, César,' she told him again. 'Thank you for loving me too.'

'Oh, hell,' he gritted as his firm stride faltered. 'If you don't stop saying things like that I'll take you right here on the stairs!'

'Sorry,' she said, her blue eyes alight with pure female mischief, her white teeth pressing into the sensual fullness of her bottom lip. 'I just wanted to say it, that's all.'

'*Santa María!*' he rasped out explosively as he entered the bedroom and toppled them both onto the bed. 'I have never known a woman affect me as badly as you do!' he muttered complainingly.

'Good,' she said. 'Keep it that way. Or I'll make like Delilah and cut off your sexy hair.'

'No need to worry about it,' he said grimly as he began dragging clothes off both of them. 'I don't even exist when I am not with you.'

'You're with me now,' she murmured consolingly.

'No, I am not,' he denied, then came over her and entered her. 'Now I am with you,' he grunted in rough satisfaction.

'If this isn't real,' she groaned as she flexed to take him in further, 'I don't ever want to wake up.'

'It's real,' he assured her. 'Feel it.' He gave a thrust of his tight hips. 'Real.'

'I belong to you, don't I?'

'Of course. What kind of statement do you think I am making here?'

Tears filled her eyes, turning summer into midnight. 'I've never belonged to anyone before,' she whispered confidingly.

The real Annie Lacey, he saw, with a pain that cut deep into his breast. Like a child, she looked helplessly, vulnerably exposed. His big chest moved on a wave of fierce emotion.

'You belong,' he avowed. 'Mine.' It was hot. It was gruff and it was possessive. 'Now take hold of my hair,' he instructed tensely.

'Why?' she asked, momentarily thrown by the command.

'Because it's sexy! All right?'

She smiled, and suddenly she was no longer Annie the vulnerable child, but Annie the sensual woman, exalting in her own power. Her fingers fixed around his hair then pulled fiercely, smothering his groan of pleasurable pain as she brought his hot mouth down onto her own.

A moment later and the ribbon fell away, allowing black silk to enclose them as they lost themselves in each other.

Yes, I belong. This is real, was Annie's last coherent thought. This is wonderfully, exquisitely real.

MILLS & BOON

Back by Popular Demand

BETTY NEELS

COLLECTOR'S EDITION

A collector's edition of favourite titles from one of the world's best-loved romance authors.

Mills & Boon are proud to bring back these sought after titles, now reissued in beautifully matching volumes and presented as one cherished collection.

Don't miss these unforgettable titles, coming next month:

Title #5   OFF WITH THE OLD LOVE
Title #6   STARS THROUGH THE MIST

Available wherever
Mills & Boon books are sold

Available from WH Smith, John Menzies, Forbuoys, Martins, Tesco, Asda, Safeway and other paperback stockists.

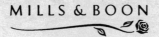

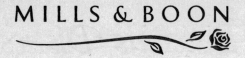

MILLS & BOON

Next Month's Romances

Each month you can choose from a wide variety of romance with Mills & Boon. Below are the new titles to look out for next month.

MISCHIEF AND MARRIAGE	Emma Darcy
DESERT MISTRESS	Helen Bianchin
RECKLESS CONDUCT	Susan Napier
RAUL'S REVENGE	Jacqueline Baird
DECEIVED	Sara Craven
DREAM WEDDING	Helen Brooks
THE DUKE'S WIFE	Stephanie Howard
PLAYBOY LOVER	Lindsay Armstrong
SCARLET LADY	Sara Wood
THE BEST MAN	Shannon Waverly
AN INCONVENIENT HUSBAND	Karen van der Zee
WYOMING WEDDING	Barbara McMahon
SOMETHING OLD, SOMETHING NEW	
	Catherine Leigh
TIES THAT BLIND	Leigh Michaels
BEGUILED AND BEDAZZLED	Victoria Gordon
SMOKE WITHOUT FIRE	Joanna Neil

Delicious Dishes

Would you like to win a year's supply of simply irresistible romances? Well, you can and they're FREE! Simply match the dish to its country of origin and send your answers to us by 31st December 1996. The first 5 correct entries picked after the closing date will win a year's supply of Temptation novels (four books every month—worth over £100). What could be easier?

A	LASAGNE			GERMANY
B	KORMA			GREECE
C	SUSHI			FRANCE
D	BACLAVA			ENGLAND
E	PAELLA			MEXICO
F	HAGGIS			INDIA
G	SHEPHERD'S PIE			SPAIN
H	COQ AU VIN			SCOTLAND
I	SAUERKRAUT			JAPAN
J	TACOS			ITALY

Please turn over for details of how to enter 👉

How to enter

Listed in the left hand column overleaf are the names of ten delicious dishes and in the right hand column the country of origin of each dish. All you have to do is match each dish to the correct country and place the corresponding letter in the box provided.

When you have matched all the dishes to the countries, don't forget to fill in your name and address in the space provided and pop this page into an envelope (you don't need a stamp) and post it today! Hurry—competition ends 31st December 1996.

Mills & Boon Delicious Dishes
FREEPOST
Croydon
Surrey
CR9 3WZ